A LIFE LESS
Broken

Dear Jeanette,

Thank you so much
for your amazing gift.
I hope you enjoy
Allyn's story.

love
margaret ♡

MARGARET MCHEYZER

A LIFE LESS
Broken

Cover created by Kellie Dennis of **Book Cover By Design**
Formatted by **Max Effect**

MONSTERS CAN ONLY SCARE US
UNTIL WE FIND OUR STRENGTH

PRE-PROLOGUE

The Monsters

"**S**O WHAT DO YOU GUYS THINK WE SHOULD FEAST ON THIS weekend?" We're at the local steak house and I look over my shoulder to make sure no one can hear us.

"I've got a taste for brunette," one of the guys says as he cracks a peanut out of its shell and pops it into his mouth.

"We had three brunettes in the past two weeks. Can't we have something more exotic? I'd like a sweet-smelling Asian cunt," says our fearless leader.

I burst into laughter. He loves the Asian girls. He told us once that there's something cathartic for him about watching their faces as their flesh rips open. He said that the images of slashing them after he's fucked them, calms him for a few days and he can work better.

"What?" he says as he looks over at me.

"You and the Asians," I laugh. "Always the Asians."

"Fuck you, cunt. You love 'em too, so I wouldn't go saying too much."

I shake my head and chuckle again. He's right, though. I do like an Asian cunt, those girls are fierce in the sack. They love it, they scream for more and more, I know when I get the knife out and start playing they go absolutely wild for it.

Mmmm, yeah I could go for an Asian pussy this weekend.

"Asian take-out?" I ask as I palm myself as discreetly as I can under the table. I don't want the boys knowing that I got a hard-on thinking about slicing a girl this weekend while she's being fucked hard in the ass. Oh yeah baby.

"We haven't had a strawberry blonde for a while."

Hmmm, I think back to the last lot of girls and there was that high school girl. She was hot, and a virgin. The way she bled was just so damn beautiful.

"Hey," one of the boys says and snaps me out of my fantasy. "We've decided we want a strawberry blonde, but not that flaming red hair. She's gotta be small, with a tight, tight ass."

I nod my head.

I know what they want, I'll find them the perfect girl. Like always.

I take my vial out of my jacket pocket and hold it in the palm of my closed fist as I stand, "I'll be back in a minute, I've got an appointment with my nose," I say as I tap it and start sniffing.

"That shit's gonna kill ya," one of the boys says.

"Not in this lifetime."

I walk to the bathroom and start to think where I'm going to find the strawberry blonde they want.

I'm sure I'll find something around the shopping center. I'll just have to watch and wait.

PROLOGUE

Why I Am The Way I Am

"**P**OLICE HAVE IDENTIFIED THE BODY FOUND BURIED IN A shallow grave as sixteen-year-old Trisha Mackenzie. Trisha went missing six days ago while walking home from school. The coroner has yet to confirm the cause of death; however, there are unconfirmed reports that Trisha suffered tremendous and horrific abuse…"

My cell phone rings and I silence the radio so I can answer it.

"Hello?" I notice it's a private number.

"Allyn, I can't come in today."

"What do you mean you can't come in to work today?" I ask Jolene whose coughing and spluttering on the other end of the phone.

"Can't you hear how sick I am, Allyn? I gotta go," she says as I hear her begin to retch.

She hangs up and I stare at the cell phone in my hand. Fuck, Thursdays are always busy in the clothing store and I know I'm going to get hammered today.

I call Jason, the owner, to see if he can find a replacement for Jolene. Maybe I can borrow someone from one of his other stores. I've had three girls out sick this week, which leaves only me to work both shifts today.

I speed dial Jason's number. I hate talking to him; he seems angry all the time. I let it ring and pray my call goes to voice mail. But he picks up on the fourth ring and sounds pissed off.

"Don't tell me you're sick too?" he spits into the phone, angrier than usual.

"No I'm not, but Jolene called in sick, and that leaves just me in the shop today. Can you get another girl to come in and help, please? We're usually so busy on Thursdays."

"I'll see what I can do, but this virus is sweeping through all my stores. Go in, open up and if I can't get help, I'll come in by about lunchtime."

"Okay, I can handle it for a few hours. See you soon, Jason." He doesn't say anything else, he disconnects the call and I go to finish getting ready for my shift.

I catch the 8:05 a.m. bus that drops me directly in front of the store. It's on the outside edge of the local shopping center, down the side and to the back a little, and even though it's out of the way, it still gets a fair bit of traffic.

When I get to the store, I squat down and unlock the front roller door, then the glass door before going in and turning the alarm off. I temporarily lock the front door from the inside so I can get the float ready and run the morning reports I need before I'm due to open at 9:00 a.m.

I look outside from the counter as I'm double checking the float, and notice the clouds have closed in quickly as the sky is dark and looks eerily threatening.

I get a small, uneasy feeling in my stomach and a frisson of electricity shoots up my spine as I look around to see if there's someone watching me. My body is covered in goose bumps and a huge lump sits in my throat.

There's something off today, something that's not quite right. It's almost as if a sixth sense is telling me to look over my shoulder, and to be wary.

I clip the store's small personal alarm onto my jeans pocket and know if something happens, I only need to press it and a distress signal will go to the alarm company monitoring the store.

As I unlock the door to open the store for business, I take a cautious look around me to see if there's something that draws my attention. But I don't see anything other than the normal foot traffic and people walking around, minding their own business.

By lunchtime, I'm totally inundated with customers. A few racks of new clothing have come in, now sitting in the store room waiting for me until I get a moment to organize them.

The store phone rings just after 12:30 p.m., and even though I'm behind the counter helping a customer, I know I need to answer it.

"Excuse me please," I politely say to the customer, and reach to grab the persistently ringing phone.

"Of course." She smiles at me and I answer it.

"Rose's Fashions, Allyn speaking. How may I help you?"

"Allyn, it doesn't look like I'll make it 'til closer to four, I'm swamped and there's no way I can get there," Jason says gruffly.

Shit. I'm going to have to just keep going on my own.

"Alright, as soon as you can would be great."

"I'll try and get there sooner, but you'd better not plan on me getting there before four."

"See you soon."

I hang up and return to the customers in the store. The day is a complete whirlwind. I haven't stopped from the moment I got here. Customer upon customer, delivery after delivery, and phone calls that don't stop.

By 3 p.m., the shop finally clears and I get a chance to catch my breath and just sit for a moment. I get my sandwich and juice from the fridge in the staff break room and sit behind the counter to eat my lunch.

As I eat, I pay particular attention to the rapidly building gray clouds and notice that the darkness of the morning never really subsided. We didn't get rain or wind yet, but it's been an unrelentingly gloomy, dreary day. I feel as if I'm waiting for some unstable, dangerous force to make itself known.

That feeling of foreboding I had earlier is started to creep over me again, and little by little it's gotten stronger.

The tingle at the back of my neck returns, like millions of tiny sparks flying to touch every nerve ending in my body.

My mouth is suddenly dry and it's difficult to swallow.

My heart suddenly thrums at a pace that could rival a healthy hummingbird.

5

Something is definitely off, but I don't know what. I look at the time on the computer and see it's 3:20 p.m. Only forty more minutes and Jason will be here. I'll feel safer when he's here with me, but right now, I feel like something awful is going to happen.

Lost amid my thoughts of warnings and fear, the bell over the door startles me and a really cute guy walks in. He eyes me, and for a moment I give him a cute, flirty smile. I put my sandwich down and stand to go to him.

"Hi there, I'm Allyn. Can I help you?" I ask. Damn, he really is cute, maybe twenty-three or twenty-four. He's tall, with dark brown hair that's a little shaggy, a strong, chiseled chin and gorgeously dark, almost black eyes. His eyes are so dark that they're captivating. I don't think I've ever seen such intensity before. They're slightly bloodshot, but even so, he's really quite a good-looking man.

"My girlfriend sent me in to buy a dress she saw at one of your other stores. Apparently it's new, just came in today. But the store she went to didn't have her size."

"I just got in some new stock. If you know which dress and what size she needs, I can go take a look."

"That'll put me in her good books if you can. Um, she said it was blue and fitted over one shoulder with a strap thing that goes around her waist. She said she's a size ten." He looks at me like he has no idea.

I chuckle to myself and shake my head. "I'll go out the back and look, give me a minute. I haven't had a chance to look at the new colors or styles yet."

"Sure, take your time."

I leave him and check that the till is locked before I go into the store room, which is next to the staff break room. I open the door and look through the racks quickly but can't see any blue dresses matching his description.

I don't get a chance to leave the room.

I hear them.

I don't see them.

A cold and terrifying panic envelops me like nothing I've ever felt before.

All my earlier feelings of dread are magnified.

I try to scream, but something covers my face.

And I'm out.

"Roll the bitch over," a deep gravelly voice says.

My body hurts. My head is aching. I feel sick.

I try to open my eyes to see where I am, and when I do I get punched in the face repeatedly. I feel something crack and when I try to scream I've got something stuffed in my mouth so my voice is muted.

I can't see them because I can't properly focus. They're faceless. There's no feature I can focus on. I'm so groggy and I just can't make out their faces.

One of them pulls my bottom cheeks apart and holds me open.

And another one savagely tears into me.

Blood drips into my eye, stopping the little vision I have.

I try to fight, but my legs are tied open and my arms are roped to two posts above my head.

They're laughing as they're raping me.

I try to scream again, but only a muffled, desperate sound comes out of me.

"Shut that cunt up, will ya, Mick," the first voice grates. I notice a distinct twang in his voice, almost like a country singer. He rolls the N in his word, his tongue stays connected with the roof of his mouth for just a moment too long.

I struggle to move as much as I can, until a punch to my head sends me to a painless place.

Black.

I try to blink my eyes open, but I can't see. Everything hurts, even my eyelids. I can't open them more than a tiny slit.

I'm lying face down, and it's so cold.

I try to move my head, but I can't. It's being restrained by something. My arms, too. Nothing is moving. I feel completely weighed down, immobile. Unprotected.

I can't see. I can't move.

I can't.

Where am I?

It's black.

I try to blink.

Why am I lying on grass? Why am I wet? Is there water around me?
I don't know where I am.

"Help." My voice is tiny, hoarse. I can't even hear me.

I try to move but can't. It's hopeless. I can't even feel anymore.

"Help." Nothing more than a small sigh escapes past my lips.

Am I dead? Is this hell?

"Fuck me, it's a woman! Call 911!"

Black.

ONE

Three Years Later.

*D*ID I LOCK THE DOOR?

Are the windows shut and locked?

Where's my panic button? Fuck, where's my panic button? Where the fuck is my damn panic button?

I check my pockets and it's not there. Is it around my neck? Nope.

The sudden lump in my throat prevents me from swallowing. My hands start shaking and my body is immediately smothered in a blanket of cold goose bumps. Where is my panic button? Why can't I find it? I need it. Who took it?

My entire frame freezes.

Have they come back?

What if they took it?

Are they here?

I can't breathe. Black spots cloud my vision. I gasp for breath, my fingers tightening around my throat. I stiffen.

Fuck, they are here!

Where's my damn panic button?

I reach out to lean against the wall before I fall, and I see it.

There's my panic button, on the hallway table.

I reach over to where it lies, innocently waiting for me.

The moment my fingers touch it, my body calms. I allow myself to relax. I'm alright.

They aren't here. They didn't come back to finish me off.

I'm not dead.

I wish I was.

I survived them and what they did to me. Not without scars though. They ruined me. They broke me, both mentally and physically. The voices inside my head tell me I'm crazy. And I listen to them, because they're right.

It's been one thousand and nineteen days since they destroyed my former life. They took me, gang-raped me, and nearly murdered me. They left me disfigured, inside and out. Most days, I wish they had killed me.

I'll never have a child of my own. I'll never be able to see more than blurs out of my left eye. The top of my right ear was bitten off. My body is scarred everywhere.

They took me to a pond and dumped me in the water. They thought I'd sink. They thought I'd drown.

But I didn't. Somehow, I made it to the shore and laid there for I don't know how long. A couple going for a walk finally found me and called 911.

For ten months, I was in the hospital.

My pelvis was completely shattered. My spleen needed to be removed. My collar bones were smashed. Both my legs were broken, in four different spots. My arms were dislocated from the shoulders and both forearms were snapped. My nose was crushed. My left eye socket was completely shattered. There were bite marks and other scars from having my skin torn open with knives.

There are no mirrors in my house. I had them all taken out before I arrived home from the hospital. I also had bars installed on all the windows, replaced my doors with double reinforced steel inside the wood and had a state-of-the-art alarm system put in before I set foot back in here.

Now this is my sanctuary…and my prison.

My very own heaven and my own personal hell.

I breathe deeply to regain my control, or what little I have that hasn't been consumed by the disabling fear, and I go back to doing my usual security checks.

I look down at my hand and grip the panic button like it's my life raft in a perfect storm.

Did I check the windows?

Are the doors locked?

I may have already checked them before my mini panic attack, but I'll do it again. I need to be sure.

My legs are shaky and my heartbeat's still thrumming away at an impossibly rapid rate, but moment by moment, I begin to calm. This panic attack was more like a small hiccup, not one of my more debilitating episodes that can last hours, days, or sometimes weeks.

I take one small step in front of the other, as I begin to walk around the bottom floor of my small two-story home.

Doors, locked.

Windows, secure.

Alarm, on.

I look around the family room at the nondescript furniture and lack of decoration.

Beige. Everything I have is beige. The sofa is beige, the dining room chairs are beige, the walls and ceiling are beige. There's no color in here.

It feels exactly like my life. Color's been stripped away.

That's another thing they stole from me the day they left me for dead. They took my ability to live a life of joy and love. Now everything I see around me is beige, the color of dead grass.

The world is cruel. People are horrible. I hate people. I hate myself. I can't love anymore. It was beaten out of me.

After I was first found, my friends were supportive. But as time passed, they weren't so supportive anymore.

"Come on, Allyn, it's been a year."

"Your therapist should be helping you."

"You're stuck in the past."

"Move on, already."

Armchair psychology and platitudes. But they didn't know how it was. They couldn't even guess.

One by one, they stopped calling. One by one, they stopped trying. One by one, they left.

My parents wanted me to move back home, but I couldn't. I hated myself enough without having them look at me with pity in their eyes. I didn't want them to see me as different, to recognize what I'd become, because then I'd know that I was different. Hopeless.

Moving in here on my own might not have been the best thing for me to do. But I learned to manage, to cope, to the best of my ability.

Breath by breath, moments became hours. Hours turned into days, eventually morphing into weeks.

My phone rings and I look at the caller ID.

"Hello, Dr. Monroe," I answer recognizing my psychologist's phone number.

"Hi, Allyn. How are you today?"

"Um, I'm okay." I lie.

"Did you take that step out your back door today?" she asks.

"Not today. But I will tomorrow." No, I won't.

"Okay. As long as you tried."

"Yeah I got to the door and I even unlocked it." No, I didn't.

"Well tomorrow, I want you to open the door and just breathe in the fresh air."

"Of course." No way.

"I'll see you tomorrow, Allyn. And when I come I want you to tell me you opened the door and stepped outside."

"Okay." No.

"Bye."

"Bye, Dr. Monroe."

I hang up and look at the phone blankly. She wants me to go outside, but she doesn't understand. I haven't been outside since I came home. I can open the door to my parents and to her, but not to anyone else.

One step at a time, I make my way up to my bedroom. I lie on my back and stare up at the beige ceiling.

The monsters under my bed scream at me. They feed my fear. They keep me locked in here, and won't let me move on.

But the monsters aren't just under my bed.

They're deeply ingrained in my head.

TWO

"SHUT THAT CUNT UP, WILL YA, MICK."

It hurts. Stop. It hurts. No more. Stop. You're hurting me.

Help!

I can't breathe; I can't scream. I'm suffocating. I'm going to die. Please just stop.

No, no, please.

Please.

I begin to cry, I can't...

I can't...

No...

I sit up in bed and grasp at my throat. I'm surrounded by silent blackness.

My heart beats loudly. My breathing is ragged, and my good eye hasn't adjusted to the darkness.

Slowly I reach under my pillow and grab the handle of the knife I keep there. I grip it with such intensity and strength that I'm sure no one can pry it out of my hand.

With my other hand I reach for my panic button, hanging safely around my neck. All I need to do is press the button to call security.

·But I listen.

I hear cicadas in the huge old tree standing regal and protective outside my bedroom window.

The steps leading upstairs make a squeaky noise when you put pressure on step four and step seven, and I listen, making sure they're quiet.

The native sounds normally surrounding me haven't been interrupted.

I'm safe.

No one's in my home.

No one has come back to get me.

No one is going to hurt me again.

My fingers cramp, and I loosen my grip on my knife, returning it to its place beneath my pillow. I reach for the bottle of water I keep by my bed, unscrew it, and take a sip. Replacing the cap, I place it back on the nightstand and lie down again.

Are the windows locked?

Is the alarm on?

Yes, I know I checked these.

I checked them and double-checked them.

But did I double-check them?

I close my eyes and try to go back to sleep, because the logical part of my brain tells me I locked them.

But my fear screams at me to go check them again.

Every night, this happens.

Every single fucking night.

I swing my legs out of bed, and flip the night-light switch on. I allow my vision to adjust before I go downstairs to check the doors and the windows.

The routine is the same: check upstairs, go downstairs, and then check upstairs again before trying to go back to sleep.

Half an hour later, the fear has been placated and I can attempt to go back to sleep.

I lie in bed, this time leaving the small night light on as I stare at my beige ceiling.

What if I had been sick that day, and Jolene was the one at work?

What if Jason had been with me from midday, like he was supposed to be?

What if I had fought harder?

Why didn't I die?

What if...?

My eyes begin to close. I can feel my breathing deepen and I begin to fall back into my nightmares.

Ring.

Ring.

Ring.

I open my eyes and reach for the cordless handset on the nightstand.

"Yeah," my sleepy voice sounds hoarse.

"Allyn, can you open up please?" Dr. Monroe asks.

What time is it? I look over to the clock to see it's 9:05 a.m. I haven't slept this late for as long as I can remember

"Sure thing," I reply

Day one thousand and twenty is starting off alright. I actually slept for more than a couple of hours and I feel okay waking up.

Maybe today is the day I'll stop hating myself.

I quickly slip on some jeans and a t-shirt and take the stairs two at a time to get to the door.

I check through the peep-hole to make sure that it's Dr. Monroe and that she is, indeed, on her own. I disarm the alarm, and open the door for her.

"Morning Dr. Monroe. I'm sorry; I overslept," I tell her as she steps through the threshold into my prison.

Dr. Monroe flicks a quick look over her shoulder at me and smiles.

"That's quite alright, Allyn." She walks into my beige family room and sits in the chair she always uses when she's here, every Tuesday and sometimes Fridays.

I lock the door, set the alarm, and before I step away, I double-check it. "I'm just going to make myself a coffee. Would you like one?" I ask.

"No I'm fine, thank you. Go make your breakfast."

I walk into the kitchen, flip the switch on the electric tea kettle and mix my coffee as I wait for the water to boil. I look out the back window and my body instantly stiffens as I recognize the same sort of dark, gray sky that loomed over me that day.

The day they warned me that my life was going to change. I watch as the angry clouds move at a glacial pace over my house, seeming to give the same warning as on the day that drastically altered my life.

A chill runs along my entire body, coursing through every part of me.

I can feel it.

The change.

Something's coming and it's going to tear me apart. Force me to face my fears.

"Allyn," Dr. Monroe touches my arm and snaps me out of the thoughts consuming me. The boiling kettle is whistling.

"Yeah?"

"Where were you?"

"Drifting with the clouds."

"Were you happy?"

"As happy as I can be," I reply.

Is it? Is this the best it'll ever be for me?

Caught in a state of self-loathing, in a beige life, with a mind still imprisoned by fear?

Is this it for me?

"I'm glad to hear that, Allyn. Did you open one of your doors and let the fresh air inside?"

I stir the hot water into my mug where the instant coffee and creamer already wait for it. "No. Maybe tomorrow." Never.

"Let's go sit in the family room and talk," Dr. Monroe suggests.

I sit and slowly sip my scorching hot coffee.

"Tell me about how you slept last night."

"I went to bed and woke up this morning."

"Did you wake up during the night?"

"Yes."

"Why?"

"I had a nightmare."

"What was it about?" she asks as she scribbles in her note pad.

"The same thing as every other night. It's always the same; it's never different." It'll never be different. I can't change what happened.

"How did you handle it?"

"I panicked and then I listened. And when I checked the doors and windows I was able to convince myself that they weren't here and I was able to finally get some sleep." I put the coffee mug on the small table in front of me and I stand up. I'm tired of this charade. Our conversations are always the same.

"Will I ever recover?" I ask Dr. Monroe.

"I can't answer that question, Allyn. You need to want to help yourself." This is the answer she always gives me.

"You don't think I want to help myself?"

"It doesn't matter what I think. What matters is the progress you're making." I can feel myself becoming frustrated.

"What progress am I making?" I ask her as I start pacing.

"What progress do you think you're making?"

Fuck.

She's so damn frustrating. I'm sick of this. I don't want more questions, I want some answers.

I can't do this shit anymore.

The monsters in my head need to leave. I can't be crazy anymore. I can't do this. And Dr. Monroe isn't helping at all.

"Get out," I say without turning to her.

"But your session's not over."

"It is now, get out."

I walk back into the kitchen and wait as Dr. Monroe packs her things.

The ominous gray clouds stare down at me, taunting me with their darkness. I feel as if I'm drifting toward them. A dark light focuses on me, dragging my broken soul and fractured mind further into the black mists.

I feel nothing but constant misery and unrelenting despair.

I'm tortured by the memories that have plagued my soul every minute of every day for the last three years.

The gray clouds suck me in, the blackness in my soul keeps me there and darkness surrounds me.

My world will never be right again.

I merely exist. I will never be alive.

THREE

LOCKING THE DOOR BEHIND **DR. MONROE, I SET THE ALARM** again and go back to the kitchen. Jumping up on the counter, I cross my legs in front of me and just look.

The sky is trying to tell me something.

The evil, dark clouds that droop over my home scream at me, performing a duet with my fear that says they're not going away without taking my shredded soul with them.

But for now, I'm safe inside my refuge, just me and my own private nightmare.

I watch as the overcast sky finally breaks and water droplets fall like tears from the gray cumulonimbus. Rain doesn't just fall, it hammers the ground in sheets, with ferocity. It wants me to know that it will never go away; it will never let me rest.

I'm forever boxed into a world of shame, humiliation, and sorrow. This is the universe telling me I will never be allowed to heal.

The moments sitting on the counter transform into hours. The rain doesn't ease. The gray just turns darker.

Finally, after what could be hours of wasted time, I get up and walk into the family room.

What a stupid name for a room.

Family room.

I'll never have a family of my own. That option was brutally taken away from me. I'll never get the chance to experience being a mother, carrying a child in my body.

I'll never be able to feel the kicks of my baby as it turns and stretches inside me.

The chance to hold that precious, tiny person in my hands is gone.

Molding a baby of my own flesh and blood into a person who knows nothing but unconditional love.

That part of life has been stolen from me. Selfishly trampled on, like an ant whose life meant nothing.

Do I have no purpose now?

Does my life have no meaning?

Was that why I was selected to have my life broken? To be disfigured and destroyed.

Am I nothing more than nothing?

A life of opportunities was given to me the day I was born, and those opportunities were taken from me the day they killed my will to fight.

I walk over to the TV and lift off the sheet that covers the screen's surface, turning away before my eyes can focus on the reflection of the damaged face staring back at me.

I sit on the sofa and reach for the remote. My mind is frail and I need to distract myself before I do something that I may regret.

Or I may not.

I turn the TV on and start flipping through the channels. There's nothing interesting, nothing that can erase the horrors swamping my mind.

"The remarkable story of survival by these three courageous women is one that I'll never forget. Four months ago, Amy, Lauren, and Shannon managed to escape from eight years of being held captive by convicted rapist and pedophile Corey Traipsy. Welcome ladies, and on behalf of our viewers, I just want to say the strength all three of you have shown is nothing short of awe-inspiring."

I watch as the female host interviews them, individually and collectively. They were each kidnapped from just outside their homes and were used for the perverse and horrific sexual gratification of their captor.

"Tell us, how have you managed to survive in the outside world in the last four months? I mean it must be just so difficult to assimilate back into a normal life," the host asks with exaggerated empathy.

The three women sit together, tightly holding each other's hands, their bodies pressed close to each other. They've been beyond hell, for days, weeks, and years. I can see it in their eyes. "Um, we've all had extensive therapy with an amazing man, Dr. Dominic Shriver, and we've also had great support from our families and friends. But for us, the most important thing is the bond the three of us share. We've been witness to things that no one should ever see; we've all experienced life at the devil's hands."

"Tell us all about Dr. Shriver and how he's helped you," the host prompts.

"Dr. Shriver's help is the main reason we've been able to survive with our sanity intact."

The camera cuts to a man sitting in the audience. He's got broad shoulders, like a swimmer, and extremely dark, straight, neat hair. He simply smiles and nods once before the camera pans back to the ladies.

Those three girls are sitting on the sofa, telling their story but I'm no longer listening.

I can't even see the light after almost three years of self-hatred and fear-ruled emptiness.

They've taken their suffering and agony and turned it into power by reliving their story.

I turn the TV off and replace the sheet that always hangs over it.

I go back into the kitchen and sit on the counter, looking outside at what's now a light drizzle. The sky is still dark, but the rain has eased and it doesn't seem so angry any more.

I pick my phone up and dial 411.

"Directory Assistance," the bored voice says.

"Dr. Dominic Shriver, please," I answer.

Getting his number is easier than I thought, the operator gives it to me and I write it on the notepad I retrieve from the top drawer, just below where I'm sitting.

I stare at the number.

He helped those three women.

Can he help me? Suddenly hopeful, I dial.

"Dr. Shriver's office," a sweet female voice answers.

20

"Um, hi. Um, my name's Allyn and I'd like to see Dr. Shriver please."

"Dr. Shriver doesn't have an opening until eight weeks from tomorrow. Do you know where his practice is?"

"I can't come there. He has to come to me."

"I'm sorry, Miss, but Dr. Shriver doesn't make home visits."

My palms start to sweat and I can feel my heart pulse faster.

"Um, I um, I really um…"

A tremor sets in and my hands are now shaking.

I can't do it. I can't leave my beige home. What if they are just outside waiting for me to leave?

"I um," I shakily stutter. There's a ringing in my ears and my vision's being overrun by a dense, black haze. "I can't breathe," I struggle to say. My breathing tightens, starting to come in short, rapid gasps.

I slide off the counter and sit on the floor with my back up against the kitchen cabinet.

"I can't," I say through a tight, constricting hand clasped around my throat. Tears flood my eyes and black spots start dotting my vision.

"Hello. Can you hear me?" A deep male voice says to me over the phone.

"I… they're every… I can't…" My chest is rising and falling rapidly.

"Shut that cunt up, will ya, Mick."

"Listen to my voice. Can you lie down for me?"

"They're in…"

"Just listen to my voice. I need you to lie down right where you are. Lie down for me, I'm right here. I won't leave you. Lie down, and close your eyes." His voice has evened out and he's talking to me in a low soothing relaxed tone. "Are you lying down?"

"Y-y-y-y," I stammer through labored breathing.

"Good, now close your eyes."

I close them as I tightly hold onto the phone.

"One, two, three, four, five." With every number he counts, they get slightly longer and his tone becomes a little lower. "Six, seven. Now breathe in deeply through your nose and hold it for me." I take a huge breath in and hold it deep inside my lungs.

"Now let it out." I exhale through my mouth. "Eight, nine, ten, eleven, twelve, thirteen. Take another breath in through your nose and hold it."

His voice is so serene. I can't resist letting the baritone lull me into a calmer state. "Let it out." I expel the breath. "Fourteen, fifteen, sixteen. Tell me your name, seventeen, eighteen, nineteen, twenty, now take a deep breath in through your nose." The shaking has stopped and so have the tears. "As you let the breath out I want you to tell me your name."

"Allyn," I say as I exhale.

"Pleased to meet you, Allyn. My name's Dominic. Twenty-one, twenty-two, twenty-three. Breathe in, Allyn."

I'm calmer now. My panic is not so intense.

"Th-thank you, Dominic."

"How can I help you today?"

"I think I need you."

"I think you may be right."

"I can't leave my house, though."

"You can't or you won't."

"I… I mean I…"

"I understand, Allyn. How about tomorrow? I'm going to hand the phone back to Lauren, my receptionist, so she can get your details. I'm going to come to your house tomorrow. Is that okay with you?"

"Um, yes. And thank you."

"It's my pleasure. I'll see you tomorrow." He gives the phone back to Lauren and she takes down all my details. Dr. Shriver's office is only fifteen minutes away from my house. Lauren tells me that he'll be here at 10 a.m.

When the call is finally finished, I slowly get up and sit back on the kitchen counter to look at the afternoon sky.

The raining has almost stopped; just a light sprinkle falls from above. There are small rays of the sun poking through the dark clouds.

I see something that I haven't seen in many years, in the distance and so very faint, but still visible.

The soft happy hues of a breathtaking rainbow.

FOUR

*T*OMORROW IS HERE.

Dr. Dominic Shriver will arrive at 10 a.m. to help me begin to mend my broken life.

The accumulated pain of one thousand and twenty-one days may soon be an ache that no longer constricts my every breath.

Standing in my kitchen, leaning against the counter with one leg bent and resting on my other knee, I do what I do every morning.

And day.

And night.

I watch but I can't see.

I listen but I can't hear.

I breathe but my heart doesn't beat.

I live but I remain dead.

Bringing the mug of coffee to my mouth, I sip on the scorching liquid, heedless of how it burns my tongue. I stare at the sky above.

The monsters that pulled me toward my grave yesterday are at bay today. The gray clouds have been replaced by pillows of white, fluffy softness drifting aimlessly across a bright blue sky.

My doorbell rings and I know that Dr. Shriver is standing mere feet away from me.

I place my coffee cup on the counter and take the first significant steps I've taken in almost three years.

When I get to the door I turn the alarm off, put one hand on the lock and the other hand on the doorknob.

But...

I look through the peep hole and the man I saw on TV is just on the other side of this thick, sturdy, steel-reinforced wooden door and the outer screen door I had installed with virtually impenetrable steel mesh.

But...

My heartbeat flutters with such intensity that a shiver vibrates up and down my spine to shake my body in an uncontrollable spasm.

The doorbell sounds again.

"Hello, Allyn," he says from the other side.

But...

I can't.

I don't know him; I can't allow him into my head or my home.

What was I thinking? I'll never be normal. I'll never function as a human again.

"You must be terrified, Allyn."

My entire body is covered in goose bumps and my mouth instantly dries up. I lean my back up against the door and my head falls back as I roll my eyes shut. I can feel him on the other side of the door.

He thinks I'm crazy.

I am.

"I'm going to sit right here and talk to you. I'm not going away, and I won't leave you."

They all leave.

"You know my name is Dominic Shriver. I started studying medicine because I wanted to help the sick, but I quickly found out I was very squeamish when it came to blood and other bodily fluids," he says then follows with a deep chuckle.

A smile teases my lips.

"Then, I decided I'd like to go into mental health, seeing as my stomach couldn't really cope with regular medicine."

I turn to look out the peep hole again. I can't see him.

"My parents weren't too impressed; they kept calling me a quack. They wanted me to either practice regular medicine or go into law. My brother went into law three years after I started at medical school. So they were happy at least one son went on to become a success, as they saw it." He chuckles again.

I stand on my tiptoes to see Dr. Shriver, but he's not visible through the peep hole.

"I've been a practicing, fully certified psychiatrist for almost nine years now. I started out helping people that had addictions, but soon progressed to patients who have experienced life-altering traumas."

"Why?" I ask him as I unlock the top deadbolt.

"Because it's what I'm good at and what I enjoy. You know there's a standard line we psychiatrists hear from people all the time. Want to hear what it is?"

"Yes please," I say as I turn the doorknob and slightly open the heavy wooden door.

"If I had a dollar for every time I've heard it, well let's just say I'd have a gold-plated car." He snickers at his own words. "We always get asked 'You won't analyze me, will you?' I have to say, Allyn, I must hear that at least once a day."

"People think you'd be able to turn that off whenever you wanted?"

"Ha! I see you understand. Of course I analyze everyone I meet, even when I'm away from my practice. I don't do it because I want to, but because that's who I am."

I swing the wooden door open. Dr. Shriver's sitting on the porch with his back against the screen door. He doesn't try to turn around or even move. He sits still with his long legs outstretched in front of him, crossed at the ankles, and the back of his head up against the screen. He's wearing a beautiful-looking dark suit.

"So how do you turn it off then?" I sit on the floor and cross my legs, facing Dr. Shriver's back on the other side of the door.

"I don't. I used to try, but it kept me awake with worry, so now I've learned to let it go. If I need to speak up about something, I do. If I can offer my advice, then I do that, too. I can come across as a pompous ass, but hey, I also get to help people."

"Who helps you then? I mean, you must absorb a lot of other people's ghosts, and you can't keep doing that, can you?"

"Allyn, you bring up a very interesting question, and one I don't get asked often. But, I'm okay. Now tell me, what made you call me?"

"I really don't know. I saw you on TV yesterday. I saw those three women and how strong they are. And I thought that maybe you can help me get my strength back."

"When was it taken from you?"

I lower my gaze to the floor and begin to twist my hands together.

"Almost three years ago, Dr. Shriver."

"Oh, please! 'Dr. Shriver' makes me sound like that pompous ass I described earlier. Dominic is perfectly fine."

"Okay," I say in a small voice.

"Three years ago your freedom was taken. Have you been outside since?"

"Only from the car to the house when I came home from the hospital."

"How do you do your shopping?" he asks, not turning around.

"My parents do it for me."

"How many people come into your house?"

"My parents and the doctor that I was seeing."

"And tell me what happens if an appliance dies and you need a new one."

"That hasn't happened yet. But when it does I'll have to figure out how to get a new one into my home."

"Tell me something; have you smiled in the last three years?"

Have I smiled? Why would he ask that?

"The first and last time I smiled was about fifteen minutes ago when you were describing your feelings toward certain bodily fluids," I answer earnestly.

"Can you tell me the happiest memory you have? It can be from any time of your life, but I love details. The more you tell me, the happier my brain gets."

I stare out past Dominic to the opposite side of the street. A happy memory. I haven't thought of anything joyful in three years.

"Are you still with me, Allyn?" he asks, bending one leg at the knee and keeping the other stretched out.

"I'm here. I'm trying to think of something."

I close my eyes and everything fades away. I don't see or hear anything except for the memory of the day that my parents and I went horseback riding.

"It was my tenth birthday," I start the story. I remember standing beside the big, beautiful, brown horse. "I was supposed to have a birthday party but it was cancelled because I got chicken pox."

The magnificent horse neighed as I reached up to pat his long nose.

"Go on."

"It was three weeks later before I was well enough to have a party, but by that time it was too late. I loved horses, and I really wanted to go riding."

In my memory, his tail flicks me as I pat his coarse, short hair on his stomach. I giggle because I remember how funny it felt.

"What's amusing?"

"Mr. Boss, that was the horse's name. I remembered that he flicked me with his tail and it tickled. I had to stand on a step stool to pull myself up into the saddle. I argued with Mom, telling her I could do it. Mom kept telling me I was too short. I can still hear her saying, 'Allyn, you're not as tall as the other kids. You can't do these things on your own.' But it didn't matter to me; I wanted to try. Of course, I couldn't get up on Mr. Boss from the ground, so I used the stool."

"And what was it like once you were up there?"

"I felt like I was seeing things I'd never seen before. I felt in control and so powerful."

I inhale deeply as I close my eyes and can smell that very distinct scent of hay wafting from Mr. Boss.

"When Mr. Boss started walking around, I wanted more. By the end of the day I had him galloping fast, and I was addicted."

"Why did you want more?"

"Being on Mr. Boss I felt so safe, he understood me. And I felt so free."

"And now?"

Those two words catapult me back into the present. I blink my closed eyes open and even through my blurry vision, I see that Dominic has turned and is now sitting facing me. I didn't hear him shift positions, and a tiny wave of fear courses through me at that realization.

"Now I'm chained by fear. I feel helpless and I'm hopelessly devoted to a life of black."

"Allyn, we've been talking for a while now and it's time for me to go. But I'm going to come back tomorrow at 10 a.m. Tomorrow though, you're going to open the wooden door straight away when I knock."

"I am?" I ask.

"You are, because you want to let some color back into your life."

"I do?"

"You called me because you don't want that life of blackness anymore, Allyn."

"I don't," I whisper realizing he's right. I don't. I want that rainbow I saw yesterday shining in my world.

"I'll see you tomorrow," he says as he stands and picks up his knapsack.

I watch as he gets in his car and drives away from my house.

I stand from the cold floor and I'm suddenly shocked at the revelation.

I opened the door.

FIVE

Dominic

DRIVING AWAY FROM ALLYN'S HOME AND BACK TOWARD MY office, I'm confident that I'll be able to work with her to give her the help she needs.

She didn't even know it, but she had the palm of her hand pressing tightly at the screen door. She's so desperate to find salvation that her mind doesn't even see it anymore.

Allyn is beyond broken. She's so far removed from her own self and from life outside her skin that she struggled with just opening the door to me. When I heard her light footsteps come to the door and then her hesitation in opening it, I knew that I'll be spending many a future day sitting on her porch.

That's okay, though. When she did finally open the door I knew that one of her biggest obstacles had been overcome.

I'm sure she didn't realize it at the time, and it may take her a few hours to accept that she took back a tiny bit of freedom by opening the door and talking to me.

It took every ounce of my willpower not to turn around to see what the woman behind that beautiful, soft, tortured voice looked like.

When I asked her about her happiest memory and she began giggling about being flicked by a horse's tail when she was ten years old, I could feel she was lost in her memory of a happier time. Allyn wants to be happy. She just needs the courage and strength to reach for it.

She was transcending her misery by retreating into a world of love and happiness, back to a time that made her smile. I hope I can help her reach those moments of purity more often so she can begin to overcome her pain.

When I turned around to face her, my eyes instantly focused on her soft, petite features. Her strawberry blonde hair cascaded down her shoulders that hung limply around her breasts.

Her lips were full, tinged a perfect pink. Her alabaster skin was clearly deficient in vitamin D, and her pallor highlighted every scar on her face.

Her gray eyes are her most intriguing feature. The deep, black smudges under them tell me that she fights for her sanity every moment of the day, losing sleep to nightmares. Her left eye is slightly droopy and a little off center compared to her right eye.

I wonder exactly what those sad, stormy eyes have seen.

Lost in my impressions of Allyn, I realize I've missed the driveway of my office. I turn my BMW around, park in my reserved spot, and exit the car.

The entire time, I've been thinking about Allyn. It's her laughter that fascinates me most. The way she described Mr. Boss and her sense of independence as she was riding him. I hope one day soon, I can get her back to a place where her mind isn't captured and tortured by images of horror.

"Hi Lauren. Can you do a Google search on Allyn Sommers and get her medical records too, please," I ask my receptionist.

Lauren's been working for me for the last six years and is in her fifties.

"Sure thing, Dom." She's the only person in the world I let call me Dom, beside my parents because truthfully, I see her like my own mother.

Walking into my office, I flick the light on and take my seat behind the large grand oak desk.

I didn't take any notes while I was at Allyn's house. I committed it all to memory so that she wouldn't feel intimidated by an obvious examination. She already felt reservations about me being there. That was evident based of the length of time it took her to open that damn door.

"Here's the Google search," Lauren says as she comes through the open door.

"Thank you."

"I'm just about to request the hospital records too. But I have to say, I remember this one. She was missing for days before she was found. It was around the time a bunch of other girls went missing, were raped and ended up dead. Two girls, Allyn and one another, survived. But the other girl ended up committing suicide shortly after she was found."

"So Allyn is one of those girls," I muse, not expecting Lauren to answer.

"Yeah," she sighs. "And she was such a beautiful young girl when she was taken."

"Thank you, Lauren," I say as I begin flipping through the pages she's printed.

I immerse myself in all information Lauren's found on Allyn Sommers. She was twenty when she went missing, found three days later at a local pond. A young couple found her, barely breathing, bound, and completely naked, with horrific injuries.

The couple was interviewed by the local paper. After they found her, and called 911, the woman ran back to their car and got a picnic blanket to cover Allyn while they waited for paramedics and police to arrive. The man stayed with Allyn, talking to her and comforting her while she drifted in and out of consciousness.

The news clippings speculated about what other harm was done to her, but I'll wait for the hospital report to see how deep her scars may go.

The perpetrators were never caught, and that partially explains why Allyn lives in a constant state of suffocating fear.

A little bit of digging by Lauren also found that Allyn's an only child. When her grandparents on her mother's side passed away in a car accident, they left Allyn enough money to buy a home and survive on a tight budget for the rest of her life.

I put the pages down and lean my elbows on the desk top, weaving my fingers together for my chin to rest upon.

Allyn took the courageous first step of calling me to help her. Locked inside her home, she's barely living and only just surviving.

Her hold on life is tenuous, and she's being pushed closer and closer to the edge of a toxic oblivion.

All alone, filled with self-loathing, remorse, and haunted by the ghosts of what was taken from her, Allyn isolates herself from the world, justifiably afraid of being hurt again.

Isolating herself is her only salvation, but it's also her disease. The more she tightens the barriers around her, the more those walls will close in around her.

One day, the walls she holds so close around her will constrict to crush her, claiming another innocent, broken life, a life that could be warm and beautiful if she allows me to help her.

My office phone rings, bringing me back out of my thoughts about how to help Allyn. I know that Lauren's on the other end waiting for me to answer.

"Lauren," I say.

"Dom, Chelsea's on the phone and she says it's important." I roll my eyes at just the mention of her name.

"Alright, put her through."

I hear the beep and know I'm now connected to Chelsea.

"Chelsea," I start this awkward conversation in a steady voice.

"Dominic, we need to talk."

"No we don't, but if you feel you have something to say, I'll give you thirty seconds," I say as my knee starts bouncing beneath my grand oak desk in irritation.

"I want to come home," she whines in an annoying voice.

"No."

"Come on, baby. I've learned my lesson. I want to come back and make it up to you."

"Chelsea, what you did can never be made up to me. I told you; we're over."

"That's ridiculous. One little mistake and you're willing to throw away ten years of marriage?"

"Little?" I can feel my body beginning to vibrate inside my own skin. "Little mistake?" My heart pounds in my fucking chest and I'm holding back all the anger I want to scream at her.

"Oh come on, you have to forgive me sooner or later," she cajoles.

"I've already forgiven you. But I haven't forgotten, and I never will. We're over."

"You think serving me with divorce papers is going to stop this? My lawyer will eat you alive," her tone turns angry. I can tell just by the huffing that she's pacing, like she always does when she's fuming.

"We'll let the lawyers fight this out. Goodbye, Chelsea," I say as I hang up before her next rant can start.

My mind instantly goes back to the twenty-three-year-old woman I met this morning.

Her strength shines so brightly to me. But her soul is deeply scarred by pain and terror.

Allyn may be broken, but I need saving too.

SIX

ONE THOUSAND AND TWENTY-TWO DAYS, AND I STILL HURT. My soul continues to bleed and my heart remains encased in ice, afraid to feel.

But today I'm going to open the door. Today I'm really going to try.

Try to see the world as a little more than beige.

Try to let some color back into my fractured life.

Try to breathe without letting the ever-present tsunami of hopelessness consume me or push me further into the blackness.

I am going to try.

Looking out my kitchen window, the sky above is a brilliant blue. Brightness shines from the partially-concealed sun, illuminating things beyond sight.

Maybe one day soon, those golden rays of light will touch me. Maybe the sunlight will thaw the ice in my heart and fill my emptiness so I can be whole again.

My doorbell rings and I know Dr. Shriver has already arrived. It's only 9:50 a.m.; he's early. I walk over to the door and look through the peep hole. I can't see him.

What if it's not him?

What if it's them, and they're back to kill me?

"Allyn, you said you'd open the door," Dr. Shriver says from the other side. He must already be sitting down waiting for me.

I enter my code to turn the alarm off, unlock the deadbolt, and then position my hand on the doorknob and the second lock.

My heart beats quickly and I feel a trickle of sweat roll down the back of my neck.

I can do it.

I can open the door.

It's only a fucking door, Allyn. Just open it.

I open the door just a crack and peek outside.

Dr. Shriver is sitting on the porch, cross-legged, facing me.

"Nice of you to join me today, Allyn. Would you care to take a seat?" he says and chuckles as he holds his hand out indicating the floor on my side of the screen door

"Thank you for coming to see me again, Dr. Shriver." I sit on the floor, mirroring his pose.

"You're going to either make me feel old, or like I have a stick stuck up my pompous ass. Can you please call me Dominic?"

I let out a small laugh and nod my head at him.

"Tell me about your night. What did you have for dinner?" he asks.

For dinner? He wants to know what I ate? That's a bit...weird.

"Um, I had spaghetti."

"Did you make it?"

"Yeah, I made it. I cook a little. I'm not great at it, but I can feed myself. I like freshly-made pasta instead of store-bought, so I try and make a batch that will last me a while. I'm not a huge eater." I look past Dominic to stare out at the street.

"What's your favorite season? I love spring myself, the promise of new and exciting things happening. Rejuvenation of what lay motionless and dormant through winter."

"The only thing I don't like is bees. I'm allergic to their sting. Actually, I carry an epi-pen with me because I'm highly allergic to them. I guess my chances of becoming a beekeeper went out the window the first time I was rushed to the hospital because my airway closed off." He laughs at his own joke and I find myself smiling along with him.

"I like fall," I answer. I lower my eyes and look at the floor.

"What is it about fall that draws you to it?"

"I like to watch the leaves change color, I sit on my kitchen counter and watch every day as the leaves go from a vibrant green, through yellow, and then to a deep orange."

"Do you like the color orange?"

"Yeah, I do. My life is so colorless. I like to pretend that I'm submerged in brightness. But most times it's only for a few seconds before I'm reminded how black my life really is." I let my chin fall to my chest, weighed by the truth of my own drab words.

"What's your favorite color? I love green; I find it very serene and peaceful."

I look at Dominic and notice he's wearing a pair of dark blue jeans and a green, button-down long-sleeved shirt.

"Purple. When I was a kid I wanted a purple room. My mom and dad loved me so much that they painted my bedroom four different shades of purple. They did it when I was at school one day, and when I came home they pretended that they'd had a normal day. When I went into my room I screamed and started crying, I was so happy."

"How old were you?"

"I was twelve. I remember that day like it was yesterday. I wasn't allowed to sleep in there for a couple of nights, until the smell was gone, but it's stayed that color to this very day. Well, I assume it's still four shades of purple. I haven't been to my parents' house in…" I trail off, not wanting to finish the sentence.

"Tell me about your best friends."

"I don't have any."

Dominic stares into my eyes, knits his eyebrows together and tilts his head to the side. "I find that quite difficult to believe, Allyn. You have a very pleasant, easy personality. Why don't you have any best friends?"

"I don't have friends at all."

"Well, that definitely can't be true," he says as he uncrosses and re-crosses his legs.

"I can't be around people. They scare me. And the friends I did have left me when I…"

"When you what?"

"When I couldn't be what they wanted."

36

"And what did they want?" he asks, shifting his weight again.

"They wanted me to be normal."

"What makes you think that you're not normal?"

"I should be over what happened to me."

"According to who?"

"Well it's been almost three years. And I saw those girls on TV, that after only four months they were able to tell their story. It's been three years and I still can't get those moments out of my head." I stand and start pacing just inside the door.

"Allyn," Dominic calls to me. I look over and he's standing, too. "Allyn," he says again, as I continue walking back and forth in a vain attempt to ease my frustration.

Three damn years and my mind won't move past it.

Why?

"Allyn!" he says forcefully, dragging my attention back to him.

"Yeah?"

"There's no right or wrong here. There are no hard and fast rules about how long it takes to heal. Comparing yourself to someone else, regardless of the situation, is useless and wrong. Every situation is unique. But I suspect you already know this. And I also suspect that your environment is the one thing you can control, so you keep yourself locked away for your own peace of mind."

I stop pacing, and turn to look at Dominic.

Are his words true?

Am I so broken that the only way I can exist is to stay hidden away in my home?

Can I choose to overcome the pain and learn to face the catastrophic event that took place that overcast day?

"I want color in my life again," I say in a tiny whisper.

"I didn't hear you," Dominic says as he takes a step closer to the screen door, turns his head and angles it toward the door so he can hear me better.

"I want to be able to see more than just beige, Dominic. I want my purple back. I want the bright orange for inspiration. I don't want black inside me anymore. I need colors." I take a step closer to the door, when I reach it I rest my forehead on the mesh and close my eyes.

"I can help you."

"Please give me hope," I say in a soft voice.

"Allyn?"

"Yes." I don't lift my head to look at him.

"Today we're finished, but tomorrow…"

"Yes," I interrupt him.

"Tomorrow you open both doors."

I lift my head and look at his soft face. His features are warm and accepting.

"Tomorrow, I open both doors," I confirm, surprising myself.

SEVEN

10 A.M. ON DAY ONE THOUSAND AND TWENTY-THREE. MY DOOR
bell hasn't rung yet.

What if Dominic doesn't come today?

What if he doesn't want to help me anymore?

What if he left me?

They always leave.

Standing in my family room with my coffee cup cradled in my hands, I eagerly look toward the door.

He said he'd be here. Where is he?

I suppose it doesn't really matter, I probably wouldn't have opened the door anyway.

I'm not ready for that yet.

No I'm definitely not ready. I'm crazy if I think that I'd actually let him inside, there's no way that I'd open those doors.

It's not time to open them yet, my soul's not willing to accept it.

I turn away from the front door and am on my way back into the kitchen, when the doorbell rings.

He's here and he wants to help me.

I put my coffee cup down and walk to the door. I look through the peep hole and Dominic is standing tall on the other side.

Taking a deep breath in through my nose, I close my eyes and lean my forehead up against the heavy, brown wooden door.

"Allyn, I'd like a cup of coffee please," he says through the door, no louder than his normal speaking voice.

He knows I'm already at the other side.

"I…" I'm not sure what I want to say. I've convinced myself that I can't open the door for him. The fear is gnawing at me and the monsters' voices keep coming at full volume.

Am I stuck inside my beige world forever?

"What time is it, Allyn?" Dominic asks.

I look to the huge wall clock that's been above the hallway table since I've moved here.

"Ten minutes past ten," I answer.

"Have you had a coffee yet?"

"I was just drinking it before you knocked."

"Great, now we can have one together. Cream and sugar, please, Allyn," he says in a sure tone.

He wants to come in. He told me yesterday that I was going to the open the door and let him inside.

And I think I can do it.

It's just two doors.

I grab for the panic button that's around my neck and grasp it tight in my hand.

Okay.

I can do this.

I turn off the alarm and open the wooden door. Dominic stands slightly to the side of the screen door, clearly expecting me to open it. He smiles at me benignly as I nervously try to unlock the latch.

My hands are shaking so badly that I fumble with it.

"Do you have regular coffee or that decaffeinated shit that seems to be the all the rage?" Dominic asks as I concentrate on putting the key in.

"Um, I only drink the real stuff. I've got a coffee machine, so I'll make you a real coffee."

"Oh, you're a barista? Well, then I expect a latte. I don't drink them often, 'cause it's not really cool for a guy to order one when he's out in public with others, but seeing as you're skilled in making coffees, you can make me a latte," he says and chuckles.

He does that often, laughs at his own jokes. I find that a smile always finds its way to my lips too.

I'd go as far as to say that I've smiled more the last three days than I have in the last three years.

Before I know it, the latch has turned and the screen door is unlocked.

Fuck.

There's nothing protecting me now. I'm totally exposed, vulnerable to the tall man standing on the other side of the door.

My fingers once again grasp my panic button. I can feel the forearm of the hand holding it begin to ache because of my incredibly tight grip.

My heart races at a speed I'm all too familiar with. Sweat beads and then rolls down my back, beginning to soak my t-shirt.

Small black butterflies dance before me and I can feel myself beginning to slip into the unknown.

"One, two, three, four," Dominic starts counting. I hold onto the door jamb for balance. "Five, six, seven." His voice gets that deeper, more serene tone. "Breathe in through your nose and hold it," he instructs me.

I breathe in and hold it as I listen for Dominic to tell me to let go of the breath.

"Let it out now, Allyn," he says and I listen. My body is calming even though I haven't let go of the panic button. But I have loosened my grip on it and the black butterflies no longer crowd my vision. "Now, may I please come in so you can make me that coffee?"

With a huge lump in my throat and a parched, dry feeling in my mouth, I turn the handle.

I open the door.

I fucking open the door.

I opened the fucking door.

Pushing it wide open, I look at a man with a huge smile on his face.

We stand observing at each other. He doesn't try to come in, and I don't move aside for him.

He's waiting for me, and I'm gathering all my courage to take that final leap of faith. To allow him access inside my home, and inside my head.

I look up at Dominic and his encouraging smile hasn't faltered. He's not looming over me, trying to intimidate me. He's standing far enough back so I can close the door if I choose to.

We simply stand looking at each other, and a silent conversation passes between us.

He's giving me time and space to back away from this if I have to, and I'm trying my hardest to step aside and let him in.

He's letting me make the decision on my own.

Maybe a moment passes.

Maybe an hour.

Round and around we seem to go. I'm holding my broken life together, and he's giving me the time to adjust to his presence in my isolation.

The hole in my soul tightens and becomes that tiny bit smaller.

I step to the side and wordlessly invite Dominic inside my home, and my life.

"Now I'm hungry too, Allyn. Thank goodness I bought us some banana bread. How about that coffee?" He steps through my threshold and stands a mere two feet away.

The moment he's inside, I quickly lock the doors and turn the alarm back on.

"This way," I say as I step in front of Dominic and lead him into my kitchen.

"May I sit?" he asks as he points to the beige chairs around my kitchen table.

"Of course, please. I'll just make you your latte."

I gather the already ground coffee and start making his latte. I can feel his eyes on me. Even though my body is perpendicular to him, I can feel the piercing, penetrating look he's giving me. I also make a fresh coffee for me and when both are done, I take them over to the kitchen table.

Pulling a chair out from beneath the table, I sit, pulling my knees up to my chest and wrapping a protective arm around them.

I wait for Dominic to ask the questions I know he will ask.

He brings the coffee cup up to his lips and slightly blows on the beige liquid before taking a sip and trying it.

"What is it about coffee that you like?" He's asking about coffee? "To me a good coffee tells a story. It talks to me and describes the journey it takes from the time the coffee cherry is ruby red and ready to be picked. The hand that pulls it off the tree, who belongs to that hand and what they have to do in order to get to work every day. Then there's the drying method, where the coffee cherries are laid out in the sun and turned several times a day in order to prevent the cherry from decaying. The drying process can take weeks; did you know that, Allyn? Weeks of turning the cherries several times a day. Now how boring a job would that be?"

"But if that's what they're employed to do, then it's probably not boring to them. Especially if the money they earn from doing that goes back to feeding their families," I say as I take a newly appreciative sip of my coffee.

"You make a very good point, which will cause me to enjoy this cup of coffee even more. Milling the beans is another three-step process, and that's before we can even test or taste the coffee."

"You seem to know a lot about coffee," I comment as I continue sipping on mine.

"I know a lot about it because I found it intriguing how the humble coffee cherry can go from a deep red to create a brown liquid when mixed with water that many of us need desperately. I like knowing how and why things work the way they do."

"And what have you deduced about the coffee bean?"

Dominic smiles at me and relaxes back in his chair. "Honestly?"

"I only want the truth," I answer.

"Without this deep, full-bodied, dark brown liquid, I wouldn't be able to think properly in the morning. And I take my hat off to the men and women that pick and process the beans that make this coffee for me."

"I made that coffee you're drinking, so you should say thank you to me, too."

"Ha!" Dominic throws his back and lets out a rumbly laugh from deep inside his chest, and I find that I smile too. "Well, how rude of me! Thank you, Allyn, I very much like my coffee."

We both drink our coffees and it dawns on me – today is the third day of talking with Dominic, and he's yet to ask me anything about the cause of my condition.

"Dominic," I say as I take the last mouthful to finish my coffee.

"Yes."

"Why haven't you asked me about what happened?"

"Because when you're ready, you'll tell me."

"What if I'm never ready to tell you?"

"What ifs don't exist in my world. There are no what ifs; there's only what happened in the past, what's happening now, and what we can do to avoid something bad happening in the future."

I look away and I can feel my eyebrows furrowing together as I consider Dominic's words.

"I can avoid something bad happening in the future by never leaving my house," I say as I stare at Dominic.

"Yes, but that's not living life. It's a black existence. And we all deserve to live in color."

"Hmmm," I say to myself, thoughtful.

"But for today, you had a mini-lesson in the life cycle of a coffee bean. Tomorrow I'll be late, but I'll be here." Dominic stands and takes his knapsack off the floor. "Oh, I forgot that banana bread. Here you go," he says as he opens his bag and puts two plastic-wrapped slices of banana bread on the table. "Banana bread is best served warm with pats of butter. If you don't want to eat any tonight then save it for our coffee tomorrow."

I stand and move toward the door. I turn the alarm off and unlock both doors, opening them so Dominic can leave.

"I'll see you tomorrow," he says as he steps outside and goes to his car.

I lock the doors and reset the alarm.

I stop at the kitchen table and look at the two innocent pieces of banana bread that Dominic brought with him.

It's then that it dawns on me.

Two very significant things are happening. They're so big that I can't deny them or shut them out of my head.

I opened both doors today, and I let a new person inside.

And...black in my life just acquired a tinge of color.

EIGHT

"**I** WAS TAKEN," I BEGIN. DOMINIC SITS IN THE SAME SEAT HE'S used for over a week, and looks at me as calmly as he always has. Not judging.

"When?"

"Three years ago. It was the day that changed my life. It was also the day that my life stopped being normal."

"Normal is subjective, Allyn. It's different for everyone," he says as he continues to look at me.

"Do you want to take notes?" I ask, procrastinating, trying to avoid recounting the horror-filled story I know I'm going to have tell him.

"If you want me to, I can, but I'd prefer to just listen for now."

I simply nod and slide my coffee cup off the kitchen table. Not saying a word, I get up and go sit in the spot where I spend most my days. I perch on the kitchen counter, looking outside at a world I cannot be part of.

Today, the clouds are dark again, a deep gray that holds the promise of a heavy rainfall. They bunch together and ominously hang over my house with foreboding authority.

Are these severe storm clouds an omen that my life will be altered after today? Are they warning me to keep my mouth shut? Warning me not to attempt breaking out of my existence and try for a new life? I can't think about that now. Dominic is waiting. "That day was different. When I woke up and turned the radio on, the news was talking about Trisha Mackenzie, a young high school girl who went missing on the way home from school, and how her body had been found." I continue to stare at the gloomy, dark sky outside.

"I worked in a clothing shop at the mall. The girl who usually worked with me called to tell me she was sick and couldn't come in that day. That was right around the time that there was a virus sweeping through the city, a twenty-four hour bug."

If only I had been sick that day too.

"I called my boss to tell him that I was short-handed and needed help, but his other stores were going through the same thing." I take a sip of my coffee and tears begin to well in my eyes.

"I was so busy, but I had a pesky feeling something bad was going to happen. It was sitting there all day, in the pit of my stomach. I just knew something awful was coming. Looking back now, I should've closed the store and refused to let anyone in."

I'm not sure if Dominic is listening. I haven't looked at him. I'm so intent on remembering and trying to put words to what happened that I can't even bear to peek.

"It was a busy day with racks of new clothes coming in and the store was filled with customers, so when the boss called at midday to say he'd been caught up and wouldn't be able to get there 'til after four, I thought that since I'd already handled half the day, a few more hours wouldn't hurt me."

The first huge drop of rain lands halfway down on the window, startling me, and rolls quietly down toward the sill.

"At about 3:30 a guy came into the shop asking about a dress his girlfriend had seen at another store but wasn't available in her size. I know now that it was just a ruse to get me away from the front of the shop so no one would see me struggling or hear me screaming. How stupid was I? Why did I believe that the girlfriend sent him? Why wouldn't she want to come in herself to try it on? Probably because there was no girlfriend and it was all a plot to get to me."

I push my shaky hands through my long, lifeless hair, and wipe away a lone tear as it rolls down my cheek.

"I went out to the back room to check the racks of new clothing to look for the dress. The rest of them must have been ready nearby, because I wasn't..." The tears are freely flowing now, and my body remembers. Every sound, every smell, every small detail.

The whoosh of air being cut by a hand rapidly closing over my mouth.

The sweet smell of the chloroform-soaked rag they clamped tightly over my face.

The big, hard body that holds me against him, his arm immobilizing me.

The deep laughter of another man who stands a few feet away, looking on and encouraging the others with his mirth.

The way my body instantly knew that I wouldn't survive.

The way my brain shut down, and gave up.

The way my mind broke because it knew I was being carried to my death.

"I wasn't smart enough to know that it was all a trick. They wanted me, and they knew what they were doing."

Staring outside at the angry clouds, I watch them as the voices scream at me. They don't want me telling Dominic my story. They're bellowing harshly, and the flashes of lightning from the clouds are my warning to shut up and keep the truth hidden inside.

"When I woke up, they had my arms tied above my head and my legs spread wide open, tied to something else. My eyes were swollen almost shut so I couldn't see them, but I could hear them. And I could feel everything they were doing to me."

Bolts of lightning furiously crisscross the sky.

"They were fucking me, tearing into me."

Enraged thunder echoes all through the house.

"My body was shutting down."

Bang – another warning from the thunder.

"They were taking turns fucking me and urinating on me."

Crack – bright, clear lightning.

"They cut me."

My tears won't stop.

"They used all of me."

My body is shaking uncontrollably.

"They laughed."

"Shut that cunt up, will ya, Mick."

"They broke me."

My heart is pounding.

"They should've killed me."

I can feel my coffee coming back up.

"I wish I was dead."

Crash.

Crack.

Boom.

Crash.

The rain is hurtling down now, the clouds screaming at me. The thunder's more frequent and the sky is lit up by electricity. The violence outside reminds me of the violence of what they did to me.

"FUCK YOU!" I yell at the stormy day.

"FUCK YOU!"

I get off the counter and run to the back door.

Disarming the alarm and unlocking the door with absolution.

I don't fucking fumble. I can't stop. The storm wants me dead.

I run out the back yard and stand with my arms fully extended out.

"FUCK YOU!" I yell up at the clouds. They want me? They can fucking have me. "I'm here! Take me. Take me away. Kill me like you wanted to that day."

I feel Dominic close to me.

"I hate you," I scream. "Just fucking take me." My tears mix with the cold, angry rain battering my body.

"I can't take this anymore. I've been punished enough." I fall to my knees and grab my hair and tear at it, trying to feel something other than sorrow.

"I was supposed to die!" I cry up at the monsters in the sky.

"Take me away, please. I can't breathe anymore. Just take me." My head falls forward and my chin rests on my chest.

Let me die.

I don't care anymore.

"Help me live by letting me die." My shoulders slump and I breathe what I hope will be the last breath I ever take.

I'm in darkness, perpetual and everlasting darkness. Deep hurt, bottomless sorrow, and an eternal hopelessness. I can't hold on anymore. The hole in my heart is so large that I'm sinking further and further into the black, an overpowering ocean raging inside me.

I throw my arms in the air and open my eyes to look through the tears and the rain, totally destroyed and completely shattered.

"I can't be saved. Cocoon me in death. Just kill me."

And then I sob. Uncontrollably, tears freely falling down my face.

I struggle to breathe, not wanting to.

I don't want to take another breath.

Dominic wraps his arms around me and we collapse to the soaking ground together.

"The sun is coming, Allyn."

NINE

Dominic

I CRADLE ALLYN IN MY ARMS AND JUST LET HER CRY. SHE'S shivering, but I don't think it's from the cold rain pelting us so relentlessly.

She sobs into my chest. Her arms cling on to me and I do the only thing I can for a person screaming at God to take their pain away.

I simply hold her and let her get it all out.

I've dedicated the last ten days to gaining Allyn's trust. I've pushed her, without her even realizing I'm doing it, all while giving her space to breathe and time to tell me what she wants me to know.

Day by day, her walls have begun to crumble, the bulletproof barrier she had built so tightly around her finally melted away.

"Will I ever be able to breathe again?" she asks as her gray, tear-filled eyes look at me.

"Yes. You will be able to breathe, and eventually, you'll start to live." I smooth her matted hair down as she buries her face against my completely saturated chest.

We sit on the soggy ground, not moving. Not a damn inch.

And I don't care that we're being beaten by the storm.

The clouds keep hammering us with rain so strong and forceful that I instinctively try to shelter Allyn's trembling body with mine so she doesn't get hurt.

She's absolutely at ease in my arms and her body is pressed tightly against mine.

Allyn may have a shattered spirit, a dark, consumed mind and horrible memories that haunt her every waking moment. But there's no denying the warmth that her body emits.

She has the most beautiful, expressive gray eyes I've ever seen. They hold so much yearning for a future that's hovering just beyond her reach.

When she smiles, a small light bursts through her entire body, a light that comes from deep within her. Her body may hold onto the past, but Allyn's soul craves a future of sun and warmth.

With Allyn safely in my arms, I watch the sky above as its assault on us begins to ease. Slowly, the rain recedes, calming to a mere sprinkle.

"I'm sorry, Dominic," Allyn says but doesn't move her head from my chest.

"You have no reason to apologize."

She tightens her arms around me.

I tighten mine around her.

"You're soaked and sitting out here in the rain because of me," she mumbles.

"That's not how I see it."

Her sweet face looks up at me as she blinks the water away. "How do you see it?"

"I'm not sitting in the rain, I'm supporting you."

"I'd like to go inside now and dry off," she says as she moves out of the protection of my arms.

I let her go, but…

Instantly I miss feeling her warmth.

Allyn stands, completely soaked through, and starts in the direction of the house. She stops and looks back over her shoulder to me.

I'm standing up as she does this, and I see her – really see her as a woman – for the first time.

Her beauty shines through, lighting up gray eyes in her delicate, angelic face.

Living through her ordeal and still having any fight left in her makes her extraordinary. I see beyond the scars on her throat and face, the way her left eye droops, or even how she tries to hide her right ear because the top was bitten off.

She's an inspiration, and truly exceptional. She fights every day against the dark, not allowing it to take her over. And today, she finally smashed the bars of her own jailed mind, escaping toward freedom.

She's wonderfully stunning and doesn't even know it.

She turns back and takes the remaining few steps to go inside her house.

"Allyn," I call to her.

She stops again and turns around toward me.

"You may have come out here to yell at the world, but you took those steps. You decided to face your pain and not let it defeat you. No one made you do this." I move my hands indicating that we're outside.

Allyn retraces her steps until she's standing before me.

"It's time for me to let the broken go," she says as her eyes focus on the neckline of my t-shirt.

Her words stun me.

She's yelled and she's cried.

And now she knows it's time for her to start healing.

"I'm going to get you a towel and then I'll get changed." Allyn smiles wanly and heads back inside to her warm house.

I get to her back porch and take my drenched shoes and socks off. Picking them up, I take them to the front entrance and leave them by the door. Allyn comes downstairs carrying a large towel, hands it to me, and disappears back upstairs.

I dry off as much as I can in the guest bathroom next to the mud room. I take my clothes off and wring them as dry as I can into the sink before I put them back on and head out to the kitchen.

"Allyn, I'm going to go," I say as I see her standing in the kitchen waiting for the kettle to boil. I don't want to leave her, but I wasn't prepared for today either. She may need me right now, but I also need to give her the space to assess what's happened for herself.

"Dominic," she calls to me as I turn to get my knapsack.

"Yeah?" I turn to look at her.

"Thank you. What you did for me is just..." She doesn't finish the sentence, I think by the way she's biting her lip and her eyebrows are knitted together, she simply doesn't know how to express what she feels.

"You did it all on your own, Allyn." I pick my bag up and move toward the front door.

Allyn is right behind me. I can hear her feather-light footsteps following me.

"Tomorrow I'd like sit out in the back yard and have a coffee, as long as it's not raining," I tell her as I pick my shoes and socks up.

"I think I can do that now," she says, nodding her head.

"I'll see you tomorrow. Call me if you want to talk." I've already given her my direct numbers in case she needs me.

"Dominic?"

"What is it?" I ask as I step on to the front porch.

"You gave me the courage to open the door."

Satisfaction – and something else – surges through me.

TEN

I LOCK THE DOOR BEHIND DOMINIC AND WATCH AS HE GETS IN HIS dark red BMW and drives away. I think I see him turn back toward the house before he leaves, or maybe he didn't. Maybe it's my imagination. I do need a person in my life that I can trust...but is Dominic that person? Maybe my mind's just playing tricks on me.

While we sat outside in the pounding rain, Dominic's arms wrapped tightly around me, it felt right.

Like that's where I belong, secure in his embrace. Against his chest I felt safe and comfortable.

But I know that he's my doctor and nothing more. It probably is all in my mind.

And I'm also well aware that just because I finally was able to open that fucking door and step outside, I'm far from being healed.

I may never work right again. My heart may never reach the potential for love it once had, which could inhibit any sort of intimate relationship I may want to experience.

But with Dominic...

The way he held me against his firm torso.

How his arms felt around my body.

The way he smoothed my hair down with his big, masculine hands. He used them to soothe me, not to hurt me, like they did.

Or even the small kiss he pressed into my hair as I sobbed, crying uncontrollably into his chest. They're all things a man would do for the person he cherishes.

I'm just his patient, and he's only my doctor.

There's also the gap in our ages. I'm twenty-three, while I think that Dominic is closer to if not already forty.

The age difference is enough to set us apart.

But does age really matter?

Would it make a difference to me if I saw an older man with a younger woman, walking down the street together holding hands? I don't think so.

What really bothers me is that I don't know a lot about Dominic, and even if the attraction I imagine is real, my mind and body are too broken to be able to give him what he wants and needs.

Turning away from the door, I take myself into the bathroom and strip as I turn on the water for a hot shower.

There are no mirrors anywhere in my home, so I can't look at the disgusting, disfigured person that would stare back in the reflection.

I wouldn't be able to look at that woman and feel anything but pity for her.

But when I look down at my body, I can see horrid reminders of the day I was taken.

The bite marks all over my stomach have mostly faded, but I can still see the outlines of them.

There was a cut across my right breast where they sliced off my nipple and left a hole. Where I should have an areola, there is now just a surgically stitched-together lump.

I would feel pity if I could go out on the street and saw someone with a scar starting behind her left ear running down to her collar bone. Another ugly reminder that they wanted me dead, but they didn't succeed.

And the huge bite mark on my right shoulder that's still so clear I can see individual tooth marks.

My body is a walking keepsake, holding memories I can never get rid of.

Scars that tell a story I'd rather forget.

A story that still plagues me with night terrors. A story so desperately tragic, that you'd be forgiven if you doubted it was real.

But real is exactly what it is to me; my body is the proof that it happened.

In the shower, I begin to lather my hands and run them over every ridge and scar embedded in my skin.

I don't remember how I got all of them, since I was in and out of consciousness. But when I was in hospital, the nurses described them to me.

I cried.

And I wished my life had ended.

I hoped I'd be able to simply stop breathing in my sleep.

Now I stand in the shower and let the warm water wash over me as I think about the magnitude of what happened today. I fought my demons head on. I stood up and showed them that I can fight.

I showed me that I can fight.

Maybe I can leave my broken life behind and slowly let the shards of me mend.

I'll never be whole. There will always be cracks, but maybe…

Maybe I'll be okay.

I turn the water off, step out of shower, and wrap a large bath towel around my hideous body. Walking into my bedroom, I get my pajamas ready before drying myself. As I pull open my panty drawer, my eye is drawn outside. Something cobalt blue flies by. When I turn and walk to my bedroom window, the most brilliant blue jay rests on the window sill.

I stand inside, admiring the sheer beauty of its feathers. The color is so vivid and so arresting that all I can do is stand still and marvel at its splendor.

Within seconds the blue jay flies away, but I'm left with an inspiring image of the dazzling bird as it spreads its wings and soars freely through the sky.

I can't make my feet move or my brain think of anything other than that blue jay. I stand, I don't know for how long, in front of the bedroom window just looking at the spot where the bird landed.

I can't recall seeing a blue jay in the past three years.

Have they been here all along, waiting for me to notice and appreciate their beauty?

The blue jay graced me with one moment of elegance before it remembered its freedom and flew away.

Was the blue jay asking me to look at myself and assess the significance of what happened today?

Was that me, stretching my wings?

Was today my first small step to finding my own independence?

ELEVEN

*L*YING IN BED AND STARING UP AT THE CEILING, I LET MY MIND drift back to yesterday. For the first time since I came home from the hospital, I opened the door and went outside.

I didn't just walk outside, I ran outside.

I was so mad at the storm and the universe it represented that I couldn't unlock the doors fast enough to get out there and just scream at it. But is going outside again, without the rage, something I can do?

Dominic said that he wants to have his coffee outside if it's not raining, and right now I'm praying it's going to rain. However, the sun seems to be streaming happily in through my bedroom window, paying no heed to my wishes.

I'm not sure going outside today will come as easily for me. Yesterday, I was in a mindless state of fury that had me breaking down my own barriers, but today... I'm not so confident.

Getting out of bed, I wonder if the blue jay from yesterday will come back to visit. I go over to the window seat and just stare out. The majestic tree outside the window gently sways as light wind sings through its branches.

I can do this. I can break the shackles of fear that imprison me and I can try to move on. With Dominic to support me, I believe I can free myself.

I dress in jeans and a long-sleeved sweater and go downstairs to make a coffee. It's already nearing ten and I know that Dominic will be here soon. As I stand in the kitchen and look out my window, there's an uncomfortable feeling in my throat as I swallow.

Yesterday's angry rain has stopped. Today the sky is filled with blue skies and gentle, fluffy, white clouds that float so effortlessly in the atmosphere. They move against the light blue background, allowing me to breathe easy for the first time in a long time.

I'm not really sure how to feel about going outside today. It requires what now seems a bold sort of freedom, something I haven't experienced since the day I was taken. It's like a light has been lit, and now is the time for me to let that illumination guide me to a better, more hopeful place.

Sipping my coffee, I'm totally captivated by the magical mystery of the clouds. They talk to me; they yell at me; they scream at me; they soothe me.

But when they're angry, they never let me forget.

Ring.

Ring, ring.

My phone snaps me out of my preoccupation and brings me back to reality.

"Hello," I say into the phone.

"Do I get to come inside today?" Dominic says.

"Are you here already?" I go to the front door. I turn the alarm off, open the heavy wooden door, and unlock the mesh door.

We both hang up at the same time.

"I was wondering if you were going to let me in. I've been knocking for a few minutes."

"Sorry, I was just looking outside and thinking." I look down and see he's got two calico bags in his hands. "What's that?" I ask as I point to the bags.

"It's a little early for lunch, but I thought we could have a picnic."

My heart instantly pounds in my chest, bile shoots to the back of my throat and my stomach contracts in a giant knot.

"I...I... I..." I can barely speak. I run to the bathroom and throw up my morning coffee. I sit in front of the toilet bowl and dry retch as my stomach continues to spasm and hurt.

"Allyn," Dominic says as he comes into the bathroom.

I look at him and shake my head 'no' as my stomach continues heaving, even though nothing's coming up.

Dominic kneels beside me and holds my hair back as my stomach continues its ruthless rebellion.

"What happened, Allyn?" he asks as tears form behind my eyelids but don't dare break through.

"I can't go on a picnic with you."

"Why not?"

"I can't go anywhere, Dominic. I'm not ready, I'm too, too, I..." I pause to gather my thoughts. "I'm too frightened."

"I was thinking more like your backyard. It's such a beautiful day and I wanted us to sit out in the sun."

My stomach calms and my heart slows from its rapid palpitations.

"You mean you don't want to take me away from here?"

"No, Allyn." He shakes his head. "You're not ready for that. One day we'll go out, but for today I just want us to enjoy the fresh air and the sensation of the breeze on our skin. And I made my best wraps ever, I have strawberries and blueberries, and of course, cheese and crackers," he says as he smoothes my hair to the side.

"You made all that?" I ask as I stand from the floor. I go to the sink and get a spare tooth brush I keep here for emergencies.

"Not only that, but I also made my secret recipe lemonade. It's so secret that only about three million people know the recipe…alright, I cheated. I Googled how to make lemonade," he says, and throws his head back and laughs. "I'll wait for you in the kitchen." He walks out and lets me brush my teeth without watching over me.

When I'm done, I can hear Dominic humming a song. I follow the deep, hypnotic sound and find him sitting in his chair waiting for me.

"What song were you humming?"

"All Of Me by John Legend. Have you heard it?"

"No I haven't."

"I'll have to play it for you; it's truly a gorgeous song. Anyway, all I need from you is two glasses for my secret recipe lemonade and for you to open that back door so we can go outside."

I get two tall glasses from the cabinet and take slow, cautious steps to the back door. I turn the alarm off and just stand for a moment looking at the lock.

There's a battle happening in my head. Part of me wants to open the door as easily as I did yesterday. But another part is telling me that monsters can't come inside my house if I keep the door closed and stay inside.

Open it.

Keep it locked.

Open the fucking door, Allyn.

They'll come back to get you.

Open the damn door.

Never unlock it.

Dominic starts humming the same song, and the deep tone of his voice eases me back to the present.

"Do you like chicken?" he asks nonchalantly. "I hope so, 'cause I made us chicken, avocado and lettuce wraps. Well, I didn't make the bread, I bought that. But I put everything else together to make the wraps."

I look over my shoulder at him and he's standing a few feet away from me, smirking a cute little smile, waiting for me to open the door.

"I brought a picnic blanket too, so we don't need to sit on the damp grass."

I put my hand on the doorknob and close my eyes, willing myself to just open the fucking door.

"If you like, you can bring a pillow out so you can lie under the sun and soak up some of those tantalizing rays."

"I used to love the sun," I say as I lean my forehead up against the door. The cool of the wood instantly travels through my body and calms the heat pulsating through every part of me.

"And one day soon, you'll learn to love it again. Starting with today. We can just sit and have our lunch, and when we're done we'll pack up and you can come back inside. But for now we need to feed our bodies so we can nourish our minds."

I unlock the first lock.

"I was going to make," he coughs, "that is, buy, a hazelnut cake for us, but I didn't know if you have nut allergies. Do you have any sort of allergies?"

"No, not to my knowledge, but I'm not keen on a lot of red meat. I prefer chicken and turkey. And I don't like cauliflower, that stuff is just gross."

"Yeah I'm not keen on it either," Dominic says.

I unlock the second lock and crack the door open a few inches.

"I have strawberries and blueberries too. I'm hoping they haven't gotten too squashed in the bag. If they are we'll just put them in the glasses with our lemonade and call it punch."

I pull the door open further.

"Do you have a favorite cheese? I love brie, or is it camembert? Those two look and taste the same to me, I mean they're both covered in that white stuff and they both taste great. But you know what I don't like? Blue cheese. I mean they inject the cheese with that stuff to make it go all veiny. It smells like socks to me, not that I stick my nose near stinky socks or anything, but that's how I imagine dirty socks would smell."

The door is completely open now and I'm standing one small step from being outside.

I turn and look at Dominic, and his encouraging smile is trying to reassure me.

"You're so close, Allyn." His voice is gentle. "Step outside and breathe."

I lift my foot and place it on the other side of the door frame.

"Today is a good day to live," he says, but doesn't move toward me. He's doing what he always does, giving me space and letting me do this on my own terms.

"Today's a good day to finally see, Dominic." And I step entirely outside.

The sun bathes me in her bright, warm rays.

"I think here's a good spot, what do you think, Allyn?" Dominic calls from halfway down the back yard.

"Sure," I say as I walk to meet him.

He shakes the picnic blanket and spreads it out, then slips off his sport shoes to sit on it. He starts taking out all the food from one of the calico bags and lays it all out on the blanket.

"You know, food tastes better when you sit down and make

conversation with the other person," Dominic says as he gestures for me to sit opposite him.

I also slip my shoes off and sit cross-legged on the blanket facing him.

"Now regardless of how bad this tastes, you're only allowed to praise my efforts."

I find myself smiling at his silly sense of humor.

"Dominic, this tastes fantastic, I've never had anything so good," I sarcastically tease him.

"Can you at least take a bite before you say it? It makes it more believable that way."

"Do you want children?" I ask, completely changing the conversation.

Dominic coughs a little, then regains his composure.

"They've never been something that I've seriously considered. The thought has crossed my mind, but I've never been one hundred percent ready for children."

"Are you married?"

"I was, and I suppose technically I still am, at least until the divorce is finalized."

"And you didn't want a child with your wife?"

"The thought did occur to me in an abstract way, but like I said, I never really considered it. And my wife didn't want a baby so we really never discussed it seriously."

"I never knew if I wanted a child, but now I can't conceive." I look up toward the sun and close my eyes.

"Why?"

"Because of what they did. They took that away from me along with everything else they broke."

"If and when you're ready, there are always other options available if you want to be a mother. Your chances aren't totally destroyed."

I look over to Dominic who's now pouring us some of his lemonade. He hands me a glass and when I sip it, it's incredibly tart. I can't help but screw my eyes shut, and I must make a funny face because Dominic bursts into laughter.

He takes a sip and screws his face up.

"Shit, I think I forgot the sugar."

"I think you forgot the sugar, too."

"Oh well, looks like we'll have to have water then. I'll go get us some." He stands, puts his sport shoes on and goes inside to get water for us.

I look toward the house and when I look back to the picnic blanket, I'm completely speechless and totally stunned at what sits neatly beside my knee.

A single brilliant blue feather.

TWELVE

WAKING UP TODAY IS TORTURE. MY ENTIRE BODY IS ACHY; MY throat feels like I'm swallowing razor blades, and I think I have a fever.

I can't move without pain shooting through every part of me.

I can hear Dominic knocking downstairs but I can't force myself to get out of bed and let him in. I reach for my phone but the moment my hand comes out from under the blanket, a rippling cold chill washes over my body.

My teeth are chattering so hard I can hear them, and I'm shaking with the cold.

Just as I grasp the phone in my hand, Dominic calls me.

"He-he-hello," I stutter through the shivers.

"Allyn, open the fucking door. What's happening?" He sounds so worried and stressed.

"Si-sick, go aw-away," I try and say.

"Not likely, come and open the door now."

"N-n-nooo, too si-si-sick." I just can't get warm no matter how much I ball myself up.

"Open the damn door, Allyn or I'll call the police and get them to beat it down."

"Fi-fi-fine."

I drag myself downstairs and let Dominic in. The moment he is in through the door, he immediately puts his palm against my forehead and looks into my eyes.

"Have you got Tylenol?"

"K-k-kitchen," I say as I wrap my arms around myself.

"Do you want me to carry you up to bed?"

I shake my head as I start back upstairs toward my room.

"I'll be up in a moment with some Tylenol."

Slowly, I make my way back into bed, pulling all the blankets up around my chin.

I hear his heavy footsteps on the stairs.

"Here you go," Dominic says, handing me two tablets to take with a glass of water.

DOMINIC

She's shivering and she's so pale.

I sit on the edge of her bed as she swallows the two tablets and hands me back the water with most of the contents still in it.

"I'm going to make you some soup, and if that fever doesn't come down I'm taking you to the hospital."

Her eyes fly open and she's furiously shaking her head. "I ca-ca-can't…"

"If it's for your health, you can and you will."

"N-n-n-noooooo," she wails through chattering teeth.

"Allyn, I can't leave you here like this."

"I'll ca-ca-ca-call m-my m-m-mom-m."

"I'm here now and I'll look after you. But if I have to, I'll take you to the hospital myself."

She's still shaking her head, but if the time comes and she's not getting better, then I'll do what I must to ensure her safety.

"I'm going down to make you something to eat. I want you to try and sleep, okay?"

She nods and curls further into herself.

"Allyn, you can't have all these blankets on you. I need to take them off so your body cools down a little. Your fever's too high." She makes a pained mewling sound, but allows me to take all the blankets off her.

She's wearing little sleep shorts, socks, and a tank top. Her legs have got scars all over them and her top is riding up so I can see her flat stomach. There are scars and bite marks all over it. I pull her socks off and her feet feel like an inferno.

"Don't cover yourself up, okay? Let your body cool down."

"Hmmm," she moans as she turns over.

The thing I'm most worried about is pneumonia setting in. I'll stay with her and monitor her, and if I don't think she's improving I'll definitely take her to the emergency room. But being a doctor has its advantages, too.

·I go downstairs and call Lauren.

"Hi, Dom. Everything okay?" Lauren asks.

"No, Allyn is quite ill. I need you to call the pharmacy and get an antibiotic shot and a pack of penicillin ready for me. Tell them I'll bring the prescription by when you bring me the medicine. I need you to bring my stethoscope and medical bag too."

"I'll call Charlie down at the drug store, that old dog owes me a favor." She laughs. "I'll be over soon with all of it."

"Thank you, Lauren."

I go into the kitchen and start opening all the cupboards. There's not much here. Maybe her parents are due to bring her groceries, but either way there's definitely not enough here to make soup for Allyn.

I look through her fridge and find even less. But I hit jackpot in her freezer. She has some frozen home-cooked meals, two of which are labelled 'chicken soup'.

I take one out and start defrosting it in the microwave.

As I'm waiting for it I hear a huge thump from upstairs.

I run up the stairs, taking them two at a time until I'm in Allyn's room. She must have rolled and fallen out of bed because she's in a fetal position on the floor.

"Allyn," I try and wake her.

"Hmmm," she murmurs.

"Can you get up?"

"Hmmm."

I easily scoop her up in my arms and place her back on the bed. Her body is sweaty, her damp hair is all over her face, and her jaw is chattering from the fever.

I push her hair back from her face, and when I smooth it away from her cheek she leans into my touch. It's just the smallest of movements, but she definitely leans into my hand. She lets out a soft purr as she moves against me and accepts my warmth.

Fuck.

What's going on?

What does all this mean?

Fuck.

I move away from her and retreat to the door, leaning up against the jamb to watch her.

The microwave's been beeping for a few minutes, indicating that the defrost cycle has finished, so I go back downstairs to see if the soup's ready for Allyn. Stirring it around, there are still some frozen lumps left in it, so I put it back in the microwave to finish defrosting.

I hear someone at the door, and assume that it's Lauren. I open it and Lauren greets me with a huge smile and a white paper bag containing the antibiotic syringe and the penicillin tablets.

"Charlie said to take your time, but I brought your pad over so you can write the prescription out and I'll take it to him on my way back to work."

"Thank you for doing this, Lauren. She's pretty bad, but if I can get the medication and some food into her, maybe she won't need to go to the hospital. You'll need to cancel the rest of my appointments today."

Lauren walks into the house and looks around from the foyer. "Not to worry, Dom. I already did that when you called me."

The microwave sounds and I look toward the kitchen.

"It's chicken soup; she needs to eat." I answer Lauren's inquisitive eyebrows.

Lauren follows me to the kitchen as I head back to get the soup out of the microwave.

"I know it's not my business, Dom, but what are you doing?"

"I'm helping a patient."

"Is that what you're telling yourself?"

"I am." Aren't I?

"Chelsea is barely out of your life. I think you need to go out and have a bit of fun before you get serious about someone again. I mean, you don't fuck around, you don't 'play the field' as you young kids say, you don't drink, you don't smoke, you barely do anything except come to work and occasionally go out for dinner with that cute brother of yours."

"Lauren, I'm turning thirty-nine this year. I don't want to party, I don't want to go out, and I don't want any flings."

"Not to be harsh, but I doubt she'll be able to give you much of anything," Lauren says as she points upstairs to where she assumes Allyn is. "She's so badly broken, Dom."

"I don't expect anything from her. I'm merely her psychiatrist."

"Okay, Dom. I'll let you think that until your mind catches up and you finally realize what you're doing."

I look at her and tilt my head to the side.

"There's nothing to realize."

"Okay." She backs away and holds her hands up, palms facing me. "Well, can you write the prescriptions out so I can go torment Charlie? It's so much fun to screw with his head. I may even let him take me to dinner, if he's a good a boy," she says and laughs a small, evil giggle.

I write the prescription and Lauren happily takes it and moves toward the front door.

"Take good care of her, Dom."

"I will," I answer her honestly.

I let Lauren out of the front door and lock it, then take the stethoscope and the antibiotic syringe upstairs to check on Allyn. I need to examine her to determine if she needs antibiotics or this is just a cold from being out in the rain.

"Allyn," I say gently, trying to rouse her from her sleep.

"Ummm," she answers as she turns toward me.

"I need to listen to your lungs, so I need to touch you with the stethoscope."

"Okay," she murmurs and turns away so her back is to me.

I should be putting the stethoscope directly on her skin, but I don't think she's ready for that. Instead, I place it over the thin material on her back and listen to her lungs as she breathes. There's a slight rattle, which tells me she'll soon have an infection if I don't intervene.

"Allyn, I need to put the stethoscope on your chest too. Can you turn around so I can listen, please?"

"Okay," she mumbles and moves so she's lying on her back.

I put the stethoscope on her chest and she flinches in her stupor. "It's just me, Allyn. I'm listening to your lungs. I'm going to move the stethoscope to a different position," I say as I smooth her hair again, trying to reassure her that I'm not going to hurt her.

"Alright, I'm tired." She falls into a light sleep as I listen to her chest.

There's a definite slight rattle, and I need to give her the antibiotics so she doesn't end up with pneumonia. I don't think she needs the injection, the tablets should be enough.

I go downstairs to check on the soup. When I return upstairs, I bring the penicillin with me. She's still lying in the same position I left her in.

"Allyn," I softly call her.

"Yeah."

"Can you sit up for me? I've got something for you to eat so you can take some medicine."

"I don't have medicine," she says, groggy.

"No, but I got you some. Can you sit up, or do you need help?"

"I'm okay." She shuffles a little and sits up in bed. Her eyes are bloodshot and her skin is pasty and almost transparent.

I sit on the bed and she reaches for the soup.

"Nope, doctor's orders." I wink at her and lift the spoon to feed her.

"I can do it." Her objection is weak.

"I didn't say you couldn't. What I said is that I'll look after you – doctor's orders." I hold another spoonful of soup up to her lips and she smiles faintly before accepting my offering.

"I'm sorry you're stuck here. I'll call Mom to come help me," she mumbles.

"Allyn, I'm here because I want to be. Now can you eat some more soup so you can take your medicine? It's not good to take it on an empty stomach."

She has three more spoonfuls of soup then yawns. I bring my hand up to her forehead and I can tell the fever is coming down.

"I don't want anymore." She starts to slide down the bed so she can go back to sleep.

"Sorry, you can't sleep yet. You need to take these pills." I pop two penicillin tablets out of the pack and pass them to her. When she has them in hand, I pass her the bottle of water that sits on the table beside the bed, unscrewing the lid first.

She pops the pills in her mouth and swallows them with a gulp of water before lying down.

"Dominic, thank you for being here," she whispers before closing her eyes and falling into an instant sleep.

I move to sit on the chair near the bedroom window and look outside.

Allyn's trust in me is beyond anything I could ever have expected at this stage. She has allowed me into her home while she remained in bed, completely vulnerable. She ate from a spoon that I held and she took medication from me without questioning what it was.

She may not know it yet, but she's begun to embrace her healing with open arms.

My gaze goes to the lovely blue sky outside and I think about the promise of a happy future for Allyn.

Just then a blue jay lands on the window sill and looks inside.

What an intense and incredible color.

THIRTEEN

*T*HE SUN IS FLOWING IN THROUGH THE WINDOW AND SHINING
directly on my face, making me uncomfortably warm and making sleep
impossible.

When I open my eyes, I see Dominic slumped in the chair across the
room. His head is back and his mouth open, and he's softly snoring. One
leg is over the arm of the chair and his arms are crossed over his chest.

Seeing him in my room hasn't freaked me out. It's actually quite
comforting knowing he's here.

I try to slide out of bed without waking him to go to the bathroom but
the moment my feet touch the cold floor, Dominic stirs and jumps out of
the chair.

"Allyn, are you okay? Where are you going?" he says as he blinks tired
eyes.

"I'm just going to the bathroom. Sorry, I didn't mean to wake you."

"I wasn't asleep. I was just waiting to see how you're feeling."

I stand and put a hand on the footboard to steady myself, my head
suddenly woozy. "Dominic, you were snoring."

He runs his hand over his eyes and then stretches his back straight and
raises his arms above his head, almost touching the ceiling. "You going all
sassy on me? I said I wasn't asleep."

"Yeah, alright." I take a shaky step toward the bathroom, "You may want to wipe that little bit of drool away then." I gesture to his mouth and giggle to myself.

Dominic wipes at his mouth and when he finds there's nothing there, he shakes his head and grins with that cute smirk of his. I walk into the bathroom and notice that I feel so much better than I did yesterday.

When I'm finished, I go downstairs and warm up the coffee machine to make Dominic and myself a coffee.

He comes into the kitchen a few moments later and sits in the chair he's assigned to himself.

"Can I help you with anything?" he asks.

"No, it's just coffee and toast."

"That's fine with me, seeing as you really don't have anything else here. So how are you feeling today?" He comes over to feel my forehead, something that I remember he did often yesterday. Even throughout the night, he persistently checked on me.

It was strange at first that it wasn't Mom here to care for me. But Dominic is very gentle, and I've really learned to trust him in the short time he's been coming here. It just felt so natural.

"I'm better. My throat's not so sore, and my body doesn't hurt as much as it did yesterday."

"You still feel a little warm to the touch, so today you take it easy."

"Of course," I say as I look down at the cups I've gotten out.

"What is it?" Dominic asks.

"I had a dream last night and I'm just thinking about it."

"What was it about?"

"Before everything happened, I had a very best friend who I pushed away when I came home from the hospital. She tried, but I just couldn't give her the friendship she deserved, so I pushed her away until she stopped calling me."

"And what do you want to do about that?"

"I'm not sure," I begin saying. "I think I'd like to call her." I continue making the coffees.

"Then why don't you?"

"What if she's forgotten about me?" I take Dominic's latte over to him. He looks down at the coffee then looks at me before picking it up and taking a sip.

"Then you remind her."

"But what if our friendship is too far gone?" I take my coffee and sit on the chair opposite Dominic.

"Are you trying to find an excuse not to call her? Because what you're saying doesn't really make sense. It sounds like you'd rather not know than take the chance and call her."

"Hmmm," I say. I'm deep in thought, mulling over Dominic's words. Am I making excuses?

"I'll make us breakfast, Allyn. Why don't you try calling her?" He gets up to get the bread out of the bread box. "What's her name?"

"Faith. She was my best friend all through school, and even after school we were still pretty tight. Until…" I don't have to finish the sentence; Dominic knows what 'until' means.

"Well, I've got the bread in the toaster. Why don't you try calling Faith? I think her reaction might surprise you. And I'm still right here for you," he says with his back turned to me as he works on breakfast.

"Alright, I think I will."

"There's no 'I think'. Either you will or you won't. So which one is it?" he says casually, glancing at me over his shoulder.

"Okay, I can do this." I walk into the family room, sit on the sofa, and pick up the phone. I dial the only number I have for Faith. The thought of talking to her again is sending my nerves into overdrive. What if her number has changed? My palms are beginning to sweat, I'm so damn nervous.

"Hello," Faith answers.

"Faith?" I recognize her voice instantly.

"Yeah. Who's this?"

"It's Allyn." My voice breaks and tears well in my eyes. My heart is pounding.

"ALLYN!" she screams into the phone. I move it away from my ear a little, but I smile at how happy she sounds.

"Yeah, I missed you," I blurt out, not really knowing how to start this conversation.

"Oh my God! Allyn, I miss you so much. How are you? What are you doing? Where are you? Can I come over to see you?" She's firing questions at me so rapidly that my head is spinning with her enthusiasm, and it makes me laugh.

"I'm still living in my home and I think I'm doing okay."

"What's been happening? Have you been getting treatment? Are you still seeing a doctor? Have you left your house yet? Tell me everything." She pauses for a moment to allow me to talk.

"Um, I've got a new doctor, and he's really quite good. He's helped me so much, but I'm calling because I was wondering if you'd like to come over. I mean, only if it's okay with you."

"Ahhhhhh!" she screams through the phone again. "Are you crazy? Of course I want to come over, but I can't come until Sunday. Can I bring lunch and come Sunday? I can't wait, Allyn, I'm so excited." Faith always talked more than me. I'm so happy that she's going to come see me.

"Okay, well Sunday it is. Thank you, Faith. I can't wait to see you."

"I've got to go, or I'll be late for work. But Sunday I'll be at your house about eleven-ish."

We hang up and I sit on the sofa with a huge smile plastered on my face. Of course, I can't see it, but I can certainly feel it. It feels as if I haven't used some of the muscles in my face in a long time. And boy, does it feel unbelievable.

"Breakfast," Dominic calls. I merrily skip into the kitchen.

Without even thinking, I throw my arms around him and hug him tightly.

His arms come up and he returns my embrace.

Something passes between us.

I feel it.

And I'm sure Dominic feels it too.

His arms tighten around me and I automatically sink further into his encircling arms, resting my cheek on his chest.

One of his hands weaves into the hair at the nape of my neck. His thumb gently strokes the skin and I close my eyes. I take a deep breath in through my nose, inhaling his masculine aroma.

His other hand moves to press against the small of my back. My own hands gently trail up his taut back, feeling the muscles tighten slightly, then ease as I continue my slow exploration.

"Hmmm," I moan ever so slightly. It feels so right to be standing here with Dominic.

"Allyn." His voice comes out all crackly and hoarse, obviously he's tense. But he doesn't let me go, and I savor this raw, intense moment with him.

"Yeah," I whisper.

"I can't do this," he says as he lets go of me and steps away.

"I'm so sorry," I mumble and turn away to hide my shame.

I run into the downstairs bathroom and close the door before he can stop me.

"Allyn, let me in. We need to talk about this."

"No we don't. Just pretend nothing happened."

Why would he ever even look at me? My ear's bitten off; I'm covered in scars; my left eye doesn't work properly. I'm stupid to think that a man like Dominic would ever regard me as anything more than just his patient. I'm so ashamed and embarrassed.

How dumb can I be?

What an idiot. He's a very good-looking man, and at least fifteen years older than me. I can't offer him anything more than a broken body and a broken mind.

"Allyn, please open the door. I'm not leaving until you open the door."

"It was stupid, Dominic. Nothing happened, nothing can ever happen, please…" Please what? Please go away, or please stay with me? "Please, just don't shame me any more than I already am," I say through the closed, locked door.

"There's nothing to be ashamed of. I wanted it too. But I can't; I'm your doctor."

And you're hideous.

"I know. I'm so sorry. I shouldn't have hugged you," I say in a small voice.

"Please open the door." His voice is so low and serene that it's difficult not to be coerced by it.

I'm so broken. I can never have a relationship with a man. Especially not Dominic.

I take a deep breath and slowly unlock and open the door. He's leaning up against the wall opposite the bathroom.

He takes a step toward me but I shake my head and hold up my arm, palm out.

"I'm sorry I didn't break that off, Allyn. I'm the one to blame," he says as he shoves his hands into his jean pockets.

"Let's just go have breakfast and forget all about it."

"You still have to take your antibiotics to make sure your fever doesn't come back."

"Sure," I say quietly as I go and sit at the kitchen table.

Dominic and I eat in silence and I don't look at him once.

I'm so scared of what I'll see in his eyes if I allow myself a glance at him.

He's most likely humiliated at having such a disgusting, broken person as me foist myself on him. I probably repulsed him.

Why would he want me? Why would anyone ever want me?

I'm beyond repair.

If I can't stand looking at myself, how could he possibly tolerate my ugliness?

FOURTEEN

Dominic

FUCK.

I sit in my office and stare at the blank laptop screen blinking back at me.

How could I be so fucking stupid?

She hugged me, and from the moment I took her warm body in my arms, I never wanted to let her go.

Fuck.

I'm such an idiot. I've never been involved with a patient before. What makes Allyn so different?

I pick the pen up and twirl it around between my fingers, thinking about that damn hug. Her soft, small body pressed against mine, the way her breasts brushed my chest, and those small sexy moans that hummed through her as her hands trailed along my back.

I close my eyes and relive those precious few moments of us standing together with no roles, no judgment, and no doctor-patient bullshit.

Her soft, feminine curves, the citrus smell of her shampoo wafting from her hair, and the smooth skin at the nape of her neck.

My heart accelerates at the memory of how it felt to tangle my hands in her silky strands and how she responded by inching closer to me.

I feel my cock getting hard, remembering the inviting little noises she made, and the desire I felt to kiss her full, supple lips. Not aggressively, but delicately, tenderly. I wish I'd leaned down and hovered over her lips, waiting for her to signal permission to mark her as mine. I think about brushing my tongue across her beautiful mouth with a feather-light touch, telling her with my kiss that I'd give her anything she wants.

Knock, knock.

Fuck.

I snap my eyes open and notice I've been rubbing my cock through my jeans. Now I'm sporting a huge damn hard-on. Fuck.

"Yeah," I say as I slide my chair further under the desk so Lauren can't see the bulge in my pants.

She opens the door, strolls in, and sits in one of the chairs opposite me.

"Yes, Lauren, what can I do for you?" I lean my elbows on the desk, concealing my erection even further.

"I want to talk to you about Allyn," she starts.

"There's nothing really to talk about."

"You've been dedicating a lot of time to her, which I'm sure is great, because she must be making progress. But it seems as if there's something more happening between you two."

"It's not…" I start, but she holds her hand up to stop me from saying anything further.

"Now listen, I've been working for you for a while now and not once have you ever looked at a patient that way. But this one, I know there's something different about her. You beam when you come back from seeing her. You've even spent the night at her house. Yes, I know she was sick and you stayed to look after her, but there's something more to this. I know there is."

"Lauren, it's really…"

"Oh, no you don't, Dom. Don't you try to pull the wool over my eyes," she says as she points a skinny finger at me. "I'm not an idiot. I can see that you've changed. You're not as stressed out any more, especially after you come back from seeing her." Lauren stops talking and sits back in the chair, crossing her legs and looking at me, clearly expecting an answer.

What can I say?

I don't even know what's happening. How am I supposed to explain it to Lauren?

"After Chelsea and what she did to me," I begin, but look away from Lauren. I don't want to see her eyes because I don't want to see judgment coming from her. She's never been critical of me before, so it would destroy me if she thinks less of me now. "Chelsea's betrayal shattered me, Lauren. Pretending she was pregnant, going to extreme measures to fake a belly, not allowing me to touch her or be there at the ultrasound..." I trail off, just trying to gain some composure. "How much of a fucking idiot was I to believe that my wife was three months pregnant, and didn't want me to go to the ultrasound because she didn't want me in the room while they did an internal? I'm her husband and a fucking doctor – a psychiatrist, for fuck's sake – and I didn't, for one minute, think she was screwing with me."

"Because you loved her," Lauren quietly says.

"How could I be so stupid? Do you know Allyn asked me if I wanted children, and I fucking lied to her and told her that I never seriously considered having them? How do I tell her that the doctor she's trusted to help her overcome all her fears is a fucking idiot? How do I tell her that all I want is a child? How do I tell her that my wife fooled me into thinking she was pregnant just so she could continue to live off my money?"

"You didn't know what Chelsea was doing. She never gave you a good reason to doubt her before. Love puts blinders on all of us, Dom."

I feel so ashamed of myself. Lauren's sweet, motherly smile says that she doesn't think I'm a fool, just a man who was in love with his wife.

"Allyn is so pure, so beautiful and trusting, and pretty much perfect for me."

"There's also a large age gap between the two of you. That by itself is going to have repercussions if you two choose to pursue a relationship." Lauren points out one of society's obvious taboos. "Not to mention you're her doctor and she's your patient." And there's the second taboo topic.

"I know, and truthfully, I don't know if Allyn will ever be able to have a normal relationship."

"Well, that's not really your decision to make for her. You can't decide for her or tell her what you think she needs."

"No I can't, but she's not ready to face how I feel about her."

"And what do you feel for her?" Lauren asks innocently, but I know what she's doing. She's forcing me to face and admit my feelings for Allyn. I'm totally aware of her manipulation, because I do the same thing.

"It's too early to say."

"Really?" she asks in feigned surprise, almost mocking me. "Because I think you know exactly what you want, Dom."

"She's still got a long way to go." I shake my head and run my hands through my hair.

"You both may have a long way to go, but don't you owe it to yourself and to her to own whatever feelings you do have?"

"Hmmm," is all I can say and nod my head in agreement.

She rises from the chair. "I'm going home early today; Charlie is taking me out on a date. What are your plans for tonight, seeing as it's Friday?"

"Oscar and I are going out for dinner and a few drinks. Nothing too interesting," I tell her.

"Damn, that brother of yours, ummm-hmmm. If only I was twenty-five years younger. How is he?"

"He's great. He's working on some high-profile case that's got him all stressed out, which is why we're going out to dinner tonight."

"Just remember, I'm leaving in about two hours to go home and get ready for my date with Charlie." Lauren walks toward the door. Before she reaches it, she turns around and looks at me, "It'll all work out. These things have a way of finding their balance," she says, leaving me with her wise words.

I rub my hand over my face, then comb my fingers through my hair and go back to looking at my blank computer screen.

My cock has gone down, but after talking with Lauren, I'm more fucking confused then I was before.

I won't have much of a life if I have to keep lying to myself.

But...

I know that I want to hold on to whatever Allyn and I have, however delicate it is.

For now, I'll keep my feelings to myself.

FIFTEEN

"**S**HUT THAT CUNT UP, WILL YA, MICK."

It hurts. Stop. It hurts. No more. Stop. You're hurting me.

Help!

My head's under water and I'm being pulled further and further into the black, dark void. Sinking and falling, suffocating as I try and claw my way out of a sinister, demon-filled tunnel.

My eyes fly open and I take in a huge gulp of air.

My heart's beating at a dangerously rapid rate.

My eyes are blurry from the tears caused by this petrifying nightmare.

Those gruesome moments replay vividly in my mind, like I've only just survived them. The torment continues for hours, days, years.

Sitting up in bed, I stare at the barren shadows dancing all around me.

I draw my knees up to my chest and wrap my arms around them. Biting down on the flesh of my knee, I try and hold on to whatever part of me is still alive.

But I can't fight the fear.

Those evil monsters under my bed will always be there.

Their bloodcurdling voices inside my head scream that I can't escape; I can't be saved.

Why do I try to fight them?

The phone beside my bed taunts me, encouraging me to call Dominic and talk to him. To let him know that right now, I'm not in a good place.

I know I'm not okay.

But what if I could escape, get away from the monsters and their nightmares?

I wonder if I can fly, like the blue jay.

If I stretch my arms like the blue jay stretches its wings, and leap from my window, will my arms save me and let me fly away?

Will the blue jay soar beside me and guide me to another universe?

Would flying end my sorrow and finally allow me happiness?

If that were true, even for a moment, I'm willing to take the risk and let my body release its suffering.

I allow my mind a vision of freedom. Maybe I'll be fortunate enough to finally get relief from all the misery haunting me.

Finally, after three hard years, I'm making the decision to free myself from the horror of my past.

I pick up my phone, resolved to say goodbye to those who matter. To tell them that I've found my independence and I'm going somewhere I'll no longer hurt.

I dial Dominic first.

"Allyn," he answers on the fifth ring. His voice is scratchy, thick with the sleep from which I've woken him. "Are you alright?"

"I'm better than alright, Dominic. I know what I need to do to overcome them and what they did to me. And I just want you to know that I'm fine now. You won't need to come here again."

"What have you done?" His tone lowers and becomes more intense, with no trace of sleep.

"I haven't done anything," I say in a happy tone. "I'm going to fly away tonight. The blue jay will show me the way."

"Allyn, I'd really like to say a proper goodbye to you. I'm getting into my car to come to your house. Can you make me a coffee, please? I really would love to have one last latte made by the best barista I know."

I hear the beep of his key fob, and then his car starts.

"I can do that for you, but I'm really anxious to see what my next home looks like. So can you hurry up please? You know I'll really miss you, Dominic. But I'm sure my new home will be perfect for me."

"Aren't you seeing Faith in a few hours? You don't want to miss out on that, do you?"

I get out of bed and turn on the light, finding my jeans and a sweater to wear.

"I'd love to see Faith, but I think she'll be happy that I'm happy. She'll understand."

"And your parents, have you called them yet?"

"No, not yet. I was going to call Mom and Dad after I talked to you."

Finally, after almost three years, I feel like a giant weight has been lifted from off my chest. I'm able to breathe more easily now, knowing the blue jay will lead me.

"What did you have for dinner tonight?"

Dinner? He's asking about food? How peculiar, but then, he's a little strange on his best days.

"I had grilled cheese tonight, nothing too fancy. What did you have?" I ask as I go downstairs and start the coffee machine.

"I went out to dinner with my brother, Oscar. We went to this small Italian place in town. It's run by a Nonna who makes the most delicious lasagna I've ever eaten. Her garlic bread is really good, too. I was thinking I could take you there one night. It's very small and quaint and I think you'd like it."

The thought of leaving this house is no longer an issue for me. How can it be? Once Dominic and I have our coffee and I call my parents, I'm going to leave with the blue jay guiding me.

"Maybe, if I ever come back from Utopia."

"When do you think you'll come back, Allyn?"

"If Utopia is as blissful as it promises to be, maybe I'll stay there forever."

"Can you open the door for me?"

There's a knock at my door and I know that it's Dominic. I joyfully skip to the entrance and switch the porch light on. Looking through the peep hole I see Dominic standing on the other side of the screen door. I hang up from him and lay the phone on hallway table.

I turn off the alarm and open the heavy wooden door. Dominic looks simply magnificent in his black jeans and tight, deep gray t-shirt. I unlock the screen door and step aside, waiting for him to come in.

"I've just fired up the coffee machine, I'll go make us a coffee," I say as he steps through. I lock the doors and turn the alarm back on.

"Oh there's no rush. Just make me the best cup of coffee you can, seeing as I'll have to wait to get another one from you for who knows how long." Dominic goes to the kitchen and sits in his chair.

I go to the coffee machine and start making our drinks.

"I think this will do me a world of good, Dominic," I say brightly, smiling over at him.

"I can see how carefree you are right now with just the anticipation of leaving, so maybe it's something you need to do."

"Really?" I ask as I turn around and look at him. "You really think it'll be good for me?"

"Sure, but first I'd just like to talk a little about why you're so keen to leave."

I bring his latte over to him and turn back to make one for me too.

"Mmm, this is a damn good coffee, Allyn. You've outdone yourself with this one."

I feel a sense of pride that I've made Dominic happy.

I'll never be able to make him happy in any other way.

I take my latte over and sit in the beige seat I always sit in and take a sip of my coffee.

He's right; it's the best I've made.

"What made you decide to find Utopia?" he asks as he picks his coffee up and takes another sip.

"I had another nightmare, and when I woke up I finally realized that this is not the life I'm supposed to be living. So much of me died that day, that now there's nothing but ugliness left behind," I say matter-of-factly. "I was supposed to move on to the next life, but I didn't."

"What was the dream about?"

"Oh, the same one I always have. He tells Mick to 'shut that cunt up' and keeps brutalizing me as though I'm nothing, not a person, not human at all, like I don't have a heart or blood that pumps through my veins." I pick a spot on the table and just focus on it. I really don't want to relive the nightmare any more.

"And when you woke up what happened?"

"I decided that I'm going to fly away. My friend the blue jay will show me how. I have his feather here, look." I reach into my pocket but the feather's not there. Shit, I must have forgotten it next to my bed. "Hang on, it's upstairs." I jump up and run to get my feather.

A wave of sorrow hits me as my fingers touch the near-weightless feather that sits on the bedside table.

I'm not sure how long I stand holding the indigo quill, fascinated by it.

It must be a while, because Dominic comes into my room.

I don't see him. I feel him.

The warmth of his body beckons to me.

Without saying a word, he steps behind me and puts a hand on my shoulder.

Tears streak my face and my breathing becomes shallower with each breath I take.

"Allyn," his deep baritone tone pleads with me, but I shake my head. I'm not ready to turn around and face him.

"I'm right here. I won't leave you," he says in a low, confident voice.

"I just want it to end," I whisper through tears, my voice warbling.

"It's not going to end. We just have to find a way for you to manage it. To dream beautiful dreams and have sun-filled days, not to let bleak twilight nightmares torment you."

Letting the feather float to the floor, I bring both hands up to cover my face in frustration and embarrassment.

"What can I do?" I ask Dominic as I turn around and finally look at him.

"For now, you'll go back to bed, and I'm going to sleep on that chair over there." He points to the same chair he slept in when I was sick. "When you wake up, you'll introduce me to your best friend, Faith." He moves toward my bed and straightens the covers. "And Monday, you and I together will go back to where you were found."

A chill runs the length of my body. My shoulders stiffen and my stomach contracts at just the thought that I'll be stepping outside. I can't even acknowledge that he wants to take me to where that couple found me, where I should have died, but lived.

I continuously shake my head without saying a word.

"This is the step you need to take to give you the ability to escape, Allyn."

Dominic stands tall before me, his intense eyes breaking through the barriers that I've erected around me. His solemn look is not demeaning or pitying, but one of concern, nurturing. He wants to help me, wants me to trust him, and I do.

Unconditionally.

But going back to the place where I was dumped and left to die will surely push me over the edge. Can't he see that?

Maybe that's exactly what I need.

To face the past so I can overcome my brokenness.

But...

Can I?

SIXTEEN

*O*PENING MY EYES, THE FIRST THING I SEE IS THE CHAIR THAT Dominic slept in.

But he's not there.

A folded blanket and a pillow have replaced the man that should be there.

I snuggle further into my blankets, knowing that he's around here somewhere. He won't be far away; he never is.

"Are you still sleeping or are you pretending to be? Either is fine with me, 'cause if you're sleeping I get to eat your breakfast," Dominic says as he comes through the door.

I turn my head to see he's carrying my grandmother's silver tray with a plate and a cup on it.

"What's this?" I ask as I sit up in bed and lean against the headboard.

"Don't get overly excited, it's just toast with honey and a cup of tea. I couldn't figure out how to use that machine of yours so I found tea bags instead." He takes the few steps and places the tray on my lap.

"Thank you so much. I've never had anyone make me breakfast and bring it to me in bed." I lift the teacup and take a sip.

Weak, too weak. But I don't want to hurt his feelings either, so I drink it.

"Faith is due here in two hours. I'd like to duck home to get a shower and change, then come back. Is that alright with you?"

"Yeah sure," I say between bites of my toast.

"Would you like to come home with me?"

I stop chewing and look at Dominic who's now sitting in his chair. A little wave of fear flares up.

"No, I don't think I can."

"Tomorrow, we go to the pond where you were found, though, remember? That's important."

"I know." I don't want to go, but I know I need to see for myself that the place where I was found isn't evil. It won't hurt me; it was simply the place I was dumped. I can't blame the geography for the circumstances. It's as silly as me hating my favorite author because they killed a main character in their latest book.

It's just the way it is.

"I know," I confirm again. "I know," I say one last time but more for my own benefit than Dominic's.

"When you finish breakfast, do you want to come downstairs and lock the door behind me?"

I place the tray on my bedside table and get up out of bed. "I'll do it now, it'll give you more time and you won't need to rush."

Dominic follows behind me down the stairs, and I open the door to let him out.

"I'll be back before Faith arrives," he says as he steps out on to the porch.

"Dominic, thank you."

"You don't need to thank me; it really is my pleasure." He takes a step closer to me but stops himself from closing the distance between us. He shakes his head and runs his hand through his hair before silently turning and leaving.

I close and lock the screen door before he reaches his car. Dominic hesitates and looks back toward my home before pulling out onto the street, and I can't turn from watching him drive away until he's out of sight.

The doorbell rings and I fly down stairs knowing it's either Dominic or Faith.

Dominic's not back yet, but that's okay because the last two hours I've spent tidying up and getting myself ready to see Faith.

The first time she saw me after the attack, she cried. She cried for me, for what I lost, and for what I endured when those beasts brutalized me.

I don't want her to cry like that for me again, because I don't want to remember any more than I already do.

No, today is a happy day, a day where the angry, dark clouds are not allowed to show themselves.

I want just the soft, fluffy white pillows and wonderful, cobalt blue jays today.

Looking through the peep-hole, I see Dominic's standing there holding a bunch of bright, colorful flowers. I turn the alarm off and open the door and can't help breaking out in a broad smile.

I unlock the mesh door, pushing it open for Dominic to come inside.

"For you," he says as he hands me the bouquet. I bring them up to my nose and the gentle aroma drifts up before I even get to smell them.

"Thank you so much," I say as I close the door behind him and lock the screen and wood doors and reset the alarm. "They're just perfect."

"I didn't know your favorite flower, so I got what I thought you'd like."

We walk into the kitchen and I get out a crystal vase and fill it halfway with water and begin to arrange the flowers in it.

"They really are beautiful, Dominic."

"Allyn, what do you want to get from today?" Dominic asks.

"I just want to see Faith and see how she's doing," I answer as I'm arranging the subtly scented flowers.

"Is that all?"

"I know that it's time for me to start healing. I'm not sure I'll ever be like I was before, but I need to stop feeling so dead inside. I need to feel, and I can't do that if I lock myself away from the world. I'm lonely, and I miss Faith. I'm tired of feeling so ashamed and afraid. I'm tired of hating myself." I walk over to where Dominic is and place the vase in the center of the table. Sitting down opposite him, I look at him and try to imagine a world where I'm not restricted to my hidey-hole.

"To start, I need to learn to live without fear and shame." I rest my elbows on the table, close my eyes, and lean my head on my arms.

"Together, we can mend your broken life so you can breathe again." He squats down beside me and gently puts his hand on my back.

I turn my head and open my eyes to see Dominic looking at me with a smile. "I mean it, Allyn. Soon you'll be able to breathe freely." He moves the back of his hand to stroke my cheek, and in anticipation, I lean into his touch as his warm hand makes contact.

Dominic pulls away and averts his gaze as he stands and clears his throat. I've done it again.

"I know," I say trying to minimize the embarrassment of stupidly misinterpreting the signs of affection I think I see. He doesn't want me. I'm not ready to fully face that. I may never be. I manufactured that fantasy to bolster my hope. I'm fooling myself.

The doorbell rings and I leap up to answer it. I have to set all the bullshit aside until later. For now, it's about rebuilding my relationship with Faith, not whatever is happening between Dominic and me.

I walk to the door and take another deep, cleansing breath. Dominic stands beside me and gives me an encouraging smile. "You can do this, and I'll be right here."

I turn the alarm off and open the first door. I'm struck by Faith's beauty. Her long, dark hair is loose, longer than I remember, and her big, brown eyes are smiling at me with so much love. I can't get the damn screen door open fast enough, I'm so eager to get her inside and just hug her.

She's excitedly bouncing on the porch. My hands fumble with the lock and I can't seem to make them work.

"Let me," Dominic says as he moves my hands away, reassuring me with his calm demeanor and sweet smile.

I step back, and Dominic easily opens the door. Faith doesn't wait for it to open all the way before she flings it open and runs in, grabs me in a tight hug, and doesn't let me go.

My happiness is overwhelming. Tears freely fall and I hold on to Faith as if she's going to disappear the moment I let her go.

"I missed you so much, Ally," Faith says. She always called me Ally; that was her nickname for me.

"I missed you too."

We stand in the doorway, holding onto each other for an indeterminate amount of time. It's Dominic's deep voice that brings us back to reality. "I'm making fake coffee, ladies. Would you like one?"

I look over at him and roll my eyes.

"Are you Ally's new doctor?" Faith asks as she hooks her arm around my waist and we walk toward the kitchen.

"I certainly am. Dominic Shriver, pleased to meet you." He holds his hand out to Faith but she lets go of me and gives him a hug.

"You got her to call me, and for that, I owe you more than a handshake."

"She did it all herself," he says as he awkwardly pats her back and pulls away.

"I'll make us a real coffee." I walk over to my coffee machine and switch it on. "What have you been doing, Faith?"

"Oh, where to start? First, I'm working for a lawyer's office downtown as their receptionist. I started dating a really nice guy, Michael Greene. We've been together for eighteen months now. He's a cop and he's always at work. He asked me to move in last week, but I'm not too sure about that yet. I mean I like coming and going when I want."

"I'm so happy for you, Faith. It seems like things have been good for you."

"Oh, they have been. And even better now that my best friend is back in the picture. Maybe Michael and I can come over one night for dinner. I'd love for you to meet him."

I swing around and search for Dominic. He's sitting at the table, quietly leaving Faith and I to talk. But I can't say yes to Faith's request.

Dominic rises and comes to stand beside me. He takes the coffee cup I'm holding in a suddenly trembling hand and puts it on the counter.

"Are the coffees ready?"

I shake my head to him.

"Do you need the milk?"

Again I shake my head. Faith is looking at me curiously, trying to figure out what's wrong.

I can't have her boyfriend here. I'm not ready to allow another man in my own private space. Especially a man I don't know.

What if he's bad and just wants to hurt me?

My entire body starts to shake and I can feel the sweat coating my palms.

"Look at me, Allyn."

I look up into his calm brown eyes searching my own.

"This is about you and Faith. Not anyone else."

I nod listening to Dominic's words.

"This is your home. You can control who comes here." Dominic's tone lowers and he lays his hands on my shoulders. "Your home," he says again.

"Okay, this is my home." I take a deep breath and keep my eyes glued to his. "I'm safe here."

"You're safe."

"I'm safe," I say again.

"You alright?" he asks me as he continues looking at me.

I find myself less nervous and anxious with Dominic standing in front of me. I nod again.

"I'm alright. Thank you." I turn to Faith and smile, "I'm sorry about that. But I can't have Michael here. I'm not ready for that."

"I'm sorry, Ally, I didn't even think before I said anything."

"I have certain triggers. It's not your fault, Faith. How were you supposed to know?"

Dominic takes his coffee and moves off to the side to allow Faith and me to talk.

The next four hours are spent just talking with my best friend, catching up on what's been happening during the last three years. Dominic doesn't really talk much, but he does add some comments to our discussions with his odd sense of humor, making both Faith and me laugh.

When Faith leaves, I lock the doors and look over at Dominic who's sitting in the family room flicking through his tablet.

"How are you feeling?" he asks without making eye contact.

"It started out a little difficult, but I'm so happy she came over. I've really missed her."

"You did really well."

I slowly make my way into the family room and sit on the end of the sofa opposite Dominic.

"I don't know how well I'm going to do tomorrow," I admit. Truthfully, I'm terrified. I'm not sure if I'll be able to take those steps out my front door.

"I won't let you fall, Allyn."

I'm not so much afraid of falling myself, but I'm petrified that I'll drag Dominic down with me as he's trying to save me.

SEVENTEEN

*B*Y 9 P.M., I'M TERRIFIED.

All day I've been trying to control my fears about tomorrow so I don't alarm Dominic, but now I can't ignore them any longer.

I'm pacing nervously. My body is trembling, my heart is racing, and sweat pours off me.

I'm absolutely shitting myself at the thought of going back there, of returning to where I was found.

But I also know that if I can do that, that I'll be okay. With Dominic by my side, this should be easier to handle.

"You haven't sat still since dinner," Dominic says gently, leaning back into the sofa with his arm braced along the back.

"I'm really scared," I answer as honestly as I can.

"What is it you're frightened about?"

I stop pacing and can feel my eyebrows knit together as I consider his question.

"Everything. What if I remember more when we get there? What if it sends me backwards? What if it does nothing for me? The only thing I know for sure is that I'm beyond frightened and nervous."

"Those are normal things to be feeling. It's a scary thing, what we're going to do. But I think it will help you move on."

I comb my fingers through my hair and pull on the roots, just to feel something other than sheer terror.

"Fuck!" I yell out in frustration then start pacing again.

"Don't do that, Allyn. Making yourself hurt is not the answer." He stands to come toward me, and when he reaches me he gently cups my shoulders and leans down to look in my eyes. "You have so much inner strength, and you're blind to it. Your courage simply amazes me."

"You think I'm courageous?" I ask, baffled. How can he think I'm that strong?

He runs his hands slowly down my arms.

"The bravest person I know."

I lower my gaze and take a small step closer to him.

"How? I'm hideous, I cry..."

His hands go to my waist and mine instinctively rest on his biceps.

He feels so right.

So warm.

I can see his chest rising and falling quickly.

He smells so nice, so manly.

"Your mind is beautiful, your soul is exquisite, and you're simply remarkable."

A tear rolls down my cheek. I don't lift my head to look into his eyes, because I'm afraid of what I might see.

Dominic pulls me against his body and wraps his arms around me as I lay my head on his chest.

I can hear the rapid thump of his heart as it beats to a quickened pace.

Much like my own.

His hands don't move beyond the small of my back. I hold on to him tightly, not wanting to let him go.

Dominic moves his head so his face is buried in my hair and I hear him take a deep breath.

"Mmm," he lets out a small, husky moan.

With my eyes closed, lost in this intimate moment, I turn my head and brush my lips against his chest. It's a moment of weakness, a moment I wish could go on forever, although in my head, I know it shouldn't happen at all.

"Allyn," he breathlessly pants my name.

"Yeah," I answer dreamily.

"My god, um…" He stops talking. "I don't think this is a good idea." He clears his throat and releases me from his warm hold. But I don't want him to let me go.

"I'm sorry. I did it again didn't I?" I step back and look up at his beautiful face. Dominic's eyes are soft and filled with an emotion I've only seen once before. Lust.

"Please don't apologize. It's me that needs to step back and give you room to heal."

What?

It's only because of him that I'm healing, finally starting to move forward. But I understand. He's just my doctor, and no matter how much more I want him to be, that's all he is.

"I need to get ready for bed."

"I'm sleeping here tonight, Allyn. You've got a guest room upstairs, and there's a bed in it, so I'm staying."

"Why?" I ask as I step away and lean against the back of the sofa.

"Because tomorrow morning, you'll need me."

Dominic has stayed with me twice before, and right from the start it's always felt right. I've never thought of him as intruding or trying to encroach on my space.

He's perfect, just as he is.

"I'm going to bed then. Good night," I say as I move around to check all the doors, windows, and the security system.

"Good night."

I go upstairs and after a quick shower, I fall into bed, exhausted from the day.

But my mind doesn't switch off.

Tomorrow, I'm going to face one of my colossal fears. Two of them, actually. I'm going to leave my house for the first time in nearly three years. And I'm going back to my own personal ground zero.

I toss and turn, willing my mind to stop thinking. But it keeps going, full steam ahead.

The seconds tick past.

I get up and start pacing quietly around my room.

The moments blend into each other, unnoticed.

I try to calm my mind by looking out my window at the moonless, dark night.

Nothing is working; nothing can ease my dread.

"Allyn," Dominic says quietly from the other side of the door.

"Come in," I call.

He opens the door and is standing in sleep pants and a t-shirt. He must have brought clothes with him. His hair is ruffled and he looks tired.

"Did I wake you? I'm sorry," I say to him.

"You didn't wake me. I couldn't sleep. And I heard you walking around. You need to get some sleep."

I look out at the blackened night sky and remain silent.

"Allyn, what's happening?"

His footsteps come closer, stopping just behind me. I close my eyes, secretly willing him to fold me in his arms.

I desperately want him to reassure me that I'll be okay.

I need his warmth now, stronger than any need I've ever known before. I want his intensity to take me over and never let me go.

"Dominic," I whisper, knowing he'll hear me.

"What can I do for you?" I feel him standing right behind me.

"I need to feel something more than the pain."

His hand rests on my hip. I place my hand over his and mesh our fingers together.

So good.

His other hand moves across my belly, resting over my navel.

He takes a step toward me, and I can feel his entire front pressed snugly against my back. As I lean my head back on his chest, Dominic leans his forehead down against me.

Perfection.

We stand, exquisitely tangled, as the night moves on.

"I need sleep, but I don't want to be alone," I say in a soft voice.

"I'll sleep on the chair."

"Dominic," I begin as I turn in his arms, "Could you please let me try sleeping with you in my bed?"

Dominic closes his eyes and pain flickers across his face. "Come on, sweetheart." He leads me over to the bed, slides in, and opens his arms for me. Slowly, with a racing heart, I follow him to lie in the space he's made for me.

He closes his arms around me and we lie facing each other, chest to chest.

I snuggle closer and he tightens his protective circle around me.

My mouth is at the base of his throat and I can't help but press the smallest, lightest kiss to his smooth neck.

"Allyn," he says in a strangled voice.

I don't say anything, I imagine that he must be feeling the same as I am, or he wouldn't be in my bed with me right now. It's a lovely fantasy.

Moments pass as we lie together.

"I wasn't very sexually active before I was raped," I approach the subject because soon I'll have to tell him. I had only had sex with one person before that day.

"It doesn't matter what you did before, it only matters who you are now."

Dominic strokes a hand over my hair.

"You need to know." I move back to look up at him.

"No I don't, Allyn. The woman lying in my arms is the only person I care for, not any past version of her."

"One day though–" Dominic cuts me off.

"We'll talk about it then, but for now I want you just the way you are, here in my arms." He leans down and presses a tender kiss on my forehead, and against my skin, he whispers, "Goodnight, Allyn."

"Thank you."

I close my eyes and calm fills me as I drift off to sleep.

EIGHTEEN

Dominic

I WAKE WITH ALLYN'S LEG DRAPED OVER MY HIP, HER ARM OVER my waist and her groin dangerously close to my morning wood.

Damn it to hell and beyond.

My erection isn't going to go down with Allyn's body so close to me. I try to get out of bed, but Allyn emits a cute moan and moves closer to me.

Fuck.

As much as I want her – and I do – I know I can't have her.

Yet.

Today is going to be very difficult for her, and she needs me with her as her doctor, not as the horny guy thinking about all the things I want to do with her.

"Hey," she says as she moves her leg away, but nuzzles in closer to me.

Damn it cock, go down! I mentally yell at myself.

The way Allyn is lying, she can undoubtedly feel my erection against her leg. God, she feels so good. She moves her leg just a little and I close my eyes for a split second, imagining it's her soft, small hand touching my cock. Maybe she would even grip it tight and slide her hand up and down as her tongue licks the slit, collecting the pre-cum beading at the tip.

Fuck, she feels so good.

"Dominic," she says, startling me out of my damn fantasy.

"Yeah." I reach under the covers and pinch my stomach, focusing on the pain there and not on my hard cock.

"Thank you for last night. I needed that." She leans up and kisses my cheek, then leaves the bed.

"You're welcome." They aren't the words I want to say to her. I want to say, 'Damn it, Allyn. I've wanted to hold you for so long, to kiss you and make love to you.' But I can't tell her those things, because she's not ready to hear them.

She leaves the room and heads downstairs, I assume to make us coffee. And I will my cock into submission.

"Are you ready?" I ask Allyn as she nervously paces in the foyer.

"I don't think I can ever be ready for this, Dominic."

"You can do this. Just take one step." I hold the screen door open for her as she attempts to step outside, but she quickly retracts her foot.

"I can't," she says in frustration. She's deathly pale, and I can see her hands tremble as she wrings them together.

"Tell me about Mr. Boss. What color is he?" I ask her. I can see that the mention of the horse she rode for her tenth birthday, the one her mother said she was too small to climb up, instantly distracts her.

"He's dark brown, but his ears are black," she says as she stands just inside the opened doors looking out across the street.

"Would you ever want to ride him again?"

Her eyes sparkle and her lips turn up at the corners as thoughts of Mr. Boss replace her fear.

"Oh yes, I'd love to ride again," she says as she steps toward the threshold.

I reach for her hand and she takes mine without even thinking.

"How about one day I take you? I'd love to meet Mr. Boss." I close the door behind her and take the keys from her clenched hand to lock the house.

"You want to come riding with me?" We take the two steps down off her porch.

"Of course, Allyn. I'd love to do a lot of things with you." We start walking toward my car.

"I'm outside, Dominic. And I'm alright, you don't have to keep distracting me," she says in astonishment as we reach my car.

I open her door and wait until she's inside and has her seat belt on before closing it and jogging around to my side.

When I get in, I look at Allyn who's pursing her lips together and trying hard not to lose control. Her hands are still wringing together, her eyebrows are furrowed tight, and her eyes are narrowed to small slits. She's holding on with everything she's got, and I'm afraid it'll only be a matter of time before she loses her grip and completely crumbles.

But I want – no, need – to be the one who wipes her tears, who holds her hand, and who sees her through it.

No one else, just me.

I take her hand in mine and entangle our fingers as we drive to the pond where she was found.

We arrive twenty minutes later.

There are no other cars in the parking lot, so I assume we're the only ones here.

Allyn's fingers tighten around mine and I can feel her hand has become clammy. She must be struggling so hard. A wave of pride swells inside me at the courage she's showing.

Her breathing is rapid and she's chewing on her bottom lip with so much force I'm afraid she's going to draw blood.

"Are you alright?"

She simply nods without saying a word or letting go of my hand.

I sit in the car patiently, waiting to get my lead from her. Allyn's wearing a gray, long-sleeved pullover falling slightly off one shoulder, exposing her perfect, broken skin. I let go of her hand, get out of the car and walk around to her side, opening the door as I extend my hand to her.

Allyn looks at my hand and tears well up in her stormy gray eyes. She's not coping well with this, but I can't let her slide back into her broken life.

She means too much to me to let her slip away.

"Allyn, you can do this," I say in a low, gentle voice.

"I can, can't I?" She looks to me for approval. The fear is clearly visible in her face.

"Take my hand, and we'll do it together."

Allyn's hand reaches for mine, but she pulls it back to rest on her thigh. She closes her eyes and takes a deep breath in through her nose.

On her second deep breath I see a small shift in her appearance. She straightens her back and lifts her shoulders, raising her head to look out the windshield in front of her.

"I need to see it," she says with a renewed confidence as she places her soft hand in mine.

I assist her out of the car and close the door. Wrapping my arm around her waist, I pull her in against me, and we walk slowly toward where she was found.

"It's really very serene. There's not a soul in sight except for us," she says.

The ground is covered in tall, green plants with the most exquisite purple and yellow flowers. They spread as far as the eye can see and as we walk through them, we create a trail that leads from the small parking area to the pond.

The area is isolated, with tall, leafy trees protecting the privacy of those who do come here.

When we reach the pond we're still completely alone.

Allyn stops walking thirty feet from the water's edge. She's breathing even more heavily, and now her whole body is trembling.

She drops my hand and closes her eyes, but lifts her head toward the warm sun with her arms outstretched.

"My world could've ended here, but I survived." She drops her arms and she turns her head to look at me.

"You're so strong."

"I…I…" Allyn suddenly clasps at her chest. I can see how rapidly she's breathing. "Why?!" she yells at me. "Why?!" she screams again, this time to the universe at large.

I move toward her, but she holds her hand up to stop me before I can reach her.

She starts pulling at her t-shirt like it's made of fire and it's burning her skin.

"Why me? Why break me?"

She takes her shoes off and throws them to the ground.

"I want to understand, just tell me why I was chosen," she screams toward the sky.

Tears roll down her cheeks and I don't think she even notices them.

"I didn't give you my soul to break, you took it and ruined me." She unfastens her jeans and slips them down her legs.

"You killed my dreams," she cries through agonizing sobs.

I don't try and stop her. She needs to release her anger as the next step in her healing.

"You took all my choices away!" she shouts up at the sun. "I've died a thousand times but you can never answer."

She rips her t-shirt over her head and is now standing in just her panties and bra.

"Just let me understand why you did this to me."

She unfastens her bra and drops it with no care to the surrounding area.

"I can never have children because of what you did to me." And she takes off her panties.

She turns to face me and I see her for the truly remarkable woman she is.

"I'm broken and scarred. I've got nothing to offer you." She falls to her knees and hides her face in her hands, in a true and raw cathartic stance.

Allyn has finally broken and although she doesn't understand it yet, she's ready to move on.

I realize suddenly that she's my everything. Allyn's scarred beauty eclipses anything I've ever known.

I scoop up a handful of wildflowers and slowly walk to her.

I kneel in front of her and lift her chin with my fingers. I kiss her forehead and wordlessly hand her the flowers.

"They're beautiful," she says as she brings them up to her nose, brushing them over her tear-stained cheek.

"No they aren't, Allyn. They're breathtaking, just like the woman holding them."

A halo of light shines around her, as her strawberry blonde hair is enriched by the rays of the sun. God is looking at her and smiling with all

His warmth.

Allyn will heal, and I'll be right beside her, holding her hand for the entire journey. I can't leave her now.

"I'm covered with scars." She looks down at her exposed body, then back to me. My gaze doesn't falter; I keep looking at her eyes, clouded with pain.

"I don't see scars. I see a beautiful, strong, courageous woman who's lived through hell, and who's choosing to fight back."

"Look at my body, Dominic. It's not attractive." Her head falls to her chest and her shoulders slump forward.

"Sweetheart, look at me," I command gently, lifting her chin up. Her eyes find mine and I smile holding her gaze. "Your mind is magical. Your soul is pure and that's what I've fallen for. I don't give a damn about your scars; I want every part of you." I run my hand down her cheek and she turns her head to kiss my palm.

"You want me? As I am? But I can't give you what you want."

"I'll wait. There's time. We'll work on everything together, Allyn, because you're a part of me just as I'm a part of you."

"You want me...and you're willing to wait?" she asks with so much hope in her voice.

I nod and kiss her forehead.

"Can you take me home now please?"

"Of course." I scoop up her underwear, jeans, and t-shirt and hand them to her. I turn my back to give her the privacy she deserves while she dresses.

As we begin walking back to my car, Allyn reaches for my hand.

"I feel better," she says with a small smile as I open her door. She slides into the passenger side and fastens her seat belt.

Closing her door, I go to the driver's side and get in. Allyn places her hand on my thigh as I drive and she looks out the window.

"I think I'd like to go to that small Italian restaurant you were telling me about."

I nearly lose control of the car, because today has been so monumental for Allyn and me.

"I'd be happy to take you out to dinner."

Fuck. My feelings for her hit me so forcefully that I want to pull over and tell her right now.

Today has been so intense for her, so liberating that I don't want to add more intensity right now.

But in this very moment I know: I love her.

With every fiber of my being, with everything that I am, I love her.

When we get to her house, she continues to hold my hand as we walk up the path to her front door.

She opens the doors and turns the alarm off as we step inside.

But for the first time since I've known her, Allyn does something that positively stuns me.

She locks the screen door, but leaves the heavy wooden door open and walks away.

She opened the fucking door...and this time she left it open.

NINETEEN

"**W**ILL YOU STAY WITH ME TONIGHT?" I ASK DOMINIC AS WE eat dinner.

"If that's what you want, then of course I'll stay." He takes a bite of the pizza he ordered for us.

"Today was such a challenge for me. I didn't know how I was going to react when I got to the pond, and then there's you," I say shyly, not really wanting to let this subject go but not knowing how to approach it, either.

"What about me?" Dominic puts his pizza down and takes a drink of his soda.

"You like me the way I am, even though there are so many things wrong with me. I'm not beautiful; my body is marked and ruined. I'd never be able to give you children if you wanted any, and I don't even know how long it will take before you and I can try to be together...that way."

He sits up straight and takes a deep breath. Maybe I've spoken too soon.

"Allyn, I need to tell you about Chelsea. She's my soon-to-be ex-wife," Dominic says as he sits back in his chair. "She deceived me. Things weren't good between us, and she knew how much I wanted a child. So she pretended to be pregnant. She even bought a fake belly, which is ridiculous. She wouldn't let me go to the first ultrasound appointment with her. I found out later she lied to me."

I gasp completely horrified that someone could do something so cruel. If she didn't want a child she should've told him. But I can't really judge her; I only know what Dominic's telling me.

"Why would she do that?" I ask him.

"Because I have money and she wanted it, so she pretended."

"How exactly did she plan on carrying on with a fake pregnancy for nine months? There would have come a time when she would have to go into labor and deliver a baby."

"I never asked her, and I don't want to know. To me, a person that's capable of such blatant manipulation of their spouse is likely adept at other dishonest acts too. So I don't want to know how or why she thought she could pull that off. I feel like a fool for believing her and being misled."

"You had no reason to doubt her, did you?" I stand from the table and take my plate to the sink.

"Looking back at it now, I can't tell exactly how much of our relationship was true. I just don't know," he says as he stands, closes the pizza box lid, and brings his plate to the sink too.

"I can't lie to you, Dominic. And more importantly, I won't lie to you."

"I know." He stands next to me and I can't help but marvel at how his wide his shoulders are, at his taut, strong chest that I always find myself drawn to. His long-fingered hands reach out, carefully drawing me in for a protective embrace.

His breathing grows more rapid as his sturdy hands grasp my hips.

Dominic's eyes darken and he steps in, his hand brushing across my lower back.

"You're the most beautiful creature I have ever laid eyes on, both inside and out," he says softly as he leans down and kisses my right cheek. His lips stay connected to my inflamed skin and I lean into his touch.

"Dominic, would you please kiss me?"

"Yes, Allyn," Dominic's voice is strained, hoarse, yet strangely sensual.

Moving my arms up around his neck, I gently pull him down to meet my lips.

"I haven't done this in a long time," I whisper timidly when he's close.

The edges of Dominic's mouth lift as the small smile that graces his lips is reflected in his eyes.

"We'll take it slow. There's no rush. Just move away if you want to stop."

Right now, I just want to feel him. Feel his perfect, fevered lips on mine, feel myself give him control while I'm in his arms, and feel how very right this moment is.

With one hand around my lower back, he carefully runs his fingertips down my jaw, coaxing me to relax and just enjoy it. His lips expertly trail down my neck, and I move my head to the side, elongating my neck to give him more skin to touch.

"You're lovely," he mumbles as he worships my throat. With his palm slowly moving across my neck he smoothly pushes my hair away to fall down my back.

Slowly Dominic moves his head and presses a kiss to the hollow of my throat.

"Mmm." A raw sound of pleasure escapes me.

Dominic's tongue moves to caress the sensitive spot just below my ear.

"Oh God," I whisper, wanting more of this.

His hand tangles into my hair. "You have the most tantalizing lips, and I can't wait to taste them. But this succulent skin on your neck is too mouth-watering to neglect," he murmurs in my ear.

I'm caught up in delicious, foreign sensations. Feelings I never thought would happen to me again.

Every nerve ending in my body is on fire, and a shivering thrill flutters deep inside my belly. Bliss blankets me as my heart pounds, thudding inside my chest.

Dominic nuzzles my earlobe, his tongue licking and swirling.

"Just beautiful," he rumbles hungrily.

Dominic lays small, gentle kisses from my ear down my jaw, just barely touching the skin, teasing, making me want more.

I run my hands through his thick, dark hair and guide his mouth where I want it.

On mine.

His lips close over mine.

He hovers for a few seconds, as if silently asking me for permission, making sure that I'm completely ready for his affection.

"Yes," I moan, staring deep into his molten eyes.

"Are you sure?" he asks, holding back his own need.

"Yes. Show me."

And his mouth seals over mine.

He's gentle yet demanding, showing me the way through our first kiss. He eagerly sucks my bottom lip into his mouth and carefully nibbles it between his teeth, applying only the smallest amount of pressure.

He laps at my lips with his supple tongue and delicately probes my mouth. I open up, silently asking him to lead the way. He massages my tongue with his own, then traces my lips with the tip.

"Mmm." I ache for more contact, to have him closer to me.

Our kiss turns more crazed as he pulls me closer to him. His arousal is obvious to me, and I'm becoming eager for more.

"Allyn," he groans as the fire between us intensifies.

His hands move down to my bottom. He grabs the cheeks in his hands and pulls me hard against him.

Instinctively, I jump up and wrap my legs around him as he moves me back to sit on the kitchen counter.

Our kiss is more powerful now, not as slow.

It's getting out of control, too fast, and I'm not ready for that.

"Stop," I say breathlessly, pulling away from his lips.

Dominic drops his hands from my thighs and takes a step back, still breathing hard.

"I'm so sorry. I didn't mean for it to get out of hand. I'm so, so sorry. Please forgive me." He moves away from me and runs his hands through his hair then rubs them over his face. His desire is obvious. "I'm such an idiot," he curses himself as he slaps the back of the chair.

"Hey, don't say that. I wanted it to happen, but we got carried away. It was just too fast for me." Have I ruined things?

"It's not your fault, I should've stopped it." Dominic comes to stand in front of me and leans his forehead against mine, taking my hands in his.

"Did I kiss alright?" I ask nervously.

"That was the best first kiss I've ever had. You're alluring and my body is still vibrating at the thought that I just kissed you," he states so confidently. "But, more important, how do you feel?"

How the hell do I answer that?

The only way I can.

With total transparent truth.

"It was so incredible that I wanted more. You were taking me to a place I didn't think I would ever reach again. I felt so secure with you and I'd like to do that again, if it's okay with you?"

Dominic throws his head back and laughs, a full belly laugh. "It's not only okay, I'm looking forward to it." He leans down and kisses my lips but doesn't deepen it.

"I'm going to get ready for bed. I'm mentally and physically exhausted," I tell Dominic as he helps me hop down from the counter. "I'll just lock up first."

I do my usual rounds downstairs, check all the windows and doors and make sure the alarm is on. Then I go upstairs, take a quick shower and get changed in my pajamas.

When I get out of the shower, I can hear Dominic in the guest bathroom having a shower, too.

Falling into bed, I do my best to stay awake but find that exhaustion overtakes me rapidly.

I feel a dip in the bed and Dominic's strong arms pull me closer to his solid, warm body now with a beautiful, clean cedar aroma. I feel him nestle snugly into my body and I inhale deeply.

As I drowse, I think I can hear the man holding me with his firm touch humming.

"You have every part of me, Allyn." He kisses the top of my head.

Maybe I dream those words.

Or maybe they were spoken.

Either way, tonight I'll have the best night sleep I've had in three years.

All because I opened the fucking door.

TWENTY

NOT ONCE DID I WAKE UP THROUGH THE NIGHT. NOT ONCE DID I wonder whose strong arms were holding me. Not once did I worry.

Dominic stayed glued to me the entire night. I may not have woken, but I could feel the heat emanating from him as I lay securely in his arms.

From time to time I felt a small brush of damp lips from a carefully placed kiss to my cheek or the back of neck, just where the hair line meets the skin.

My eyelids flutter open as the warm rays of the sun touches my face.

I wiggle back a little and mold myself to the body of the perfect man softly snoring behind me. The moment my body becomes flush with his, he tightens his grip around my waist and splays his hand across my belly.

"Good morning, sweetheart," he murmurs in my ear. The warmth of his breath hits my already sensitive skin and it sends a welcome shiver down my back.

"Morning," I reply as I close my eyes and enjoy Dominic's all-encompassing presence.

"I love waking up with you in my arms. I could easily get used to this, Allyn." He presses a small kiss to my neck. "Mmm, so very easily." He moves the strap of my pajama top to the side and kisses my shoulder with gentle lips.

"I think I'd like that too." I tilt my head to the side and move my arm back to rest on his hip. Dominic is obviously aroused; I can feel his erection pressing into me. He doesn't move his hips or thrust into me to tell me he wants me, but I can feel his desire.

And soon I hope I'll be able to give him what he needs, find the loving part of me that they abused and destroyed and reclaim it.

But for now, I trust that Dominic won't push me into anything I'm not ready for.

His hand moves to the top of my thigh and he slowly runs it from my hip to my knee.

A small groan rumbles through his chest as he kisses down my back with the softest of touches.

The sound of that groan rips through me and I find myself becoming more aroused with every sound that resonates from deep within him.

Suddenly, what they did to me intrudes so forcefully into my mind that anything I was feeling is instantly drowned in a bucket of ice-cold water.

"No more," I say to Dominic.

He removes his hands and moves back so his body isn't touching mine at all. "Are you alright, Allyn?"

I shake my head and curl further into myself.

"Please, don't do that, sweetheart. Talk to me; tell me what happened. Did I push you too far?" he asks as he lays one hand on my arm.

"No it wasn't you, Dominic. It was memories of them. I'm just not ready for us to take that next step." How stupid am I? The most perfect man in the world lays his soul at my feet and I can't reciprocate in the way he deserves.

"It's fine. I'm in no hurry; I'm not going anywhere." He presses another kiss to my cheek and flings the blanket and sheet back as he rises and strolls out of my bedroom.

"I'm making coffee," he says as he's halfway down the stairs. That's my cue. I know he can't operate my machine, so he's going to make tea instead.

I smile at his subtle hint and get out of bed and go down to the kitchen.

"I've been thinking about something, Allyn," Dominic hugs me from behind as I turn the machine on and wait for it to reach temperature.

"And what's that?"

"I'd like us to go buy you a mirror."

I stiffen in his arms. Once I can actually see myself, I'll be even more ashamed than I am just looking down at my revolting body.

"Why?" I ask, trying to sound like it's not bothering me as much as it actually is.

"It's one more step toward your recovery. How about after breakfast we remove that sheet you have covering your TV? And I mean remove it permanently?" He burrows into me and kisses my cheek. "We'll start with that."

"Um, I think I can do that." I concentrate on making our coffees and try not to let the fear of seeing my reflection in the TV screen overtake me.

"I'm so very proud of you," he whispers and presses another kiss to my cheek. "I'm thinking of toast, or possibly toast if you're feeling adventurous, or toast for breakfast. What would you like?" He releases me and leans up against the counter beside me, our hips touching. A cheeky smile brightens his face.

"Hmmm, let me see." I tap my finger to my lips and scrunch my eyebrows together pretending that it's a difficult decision. "I think I'll take option A please. I'll lock in toast."

Dominic's playful smile grows even bigger as he sets about making our breakfast.

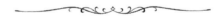

We stand in front of the TV and I look at the red fabric that covers it, concealing my disgusting scars from my vision.

"Are you ready?" Dominic asks as he weaves our fingers together.

I shake my head. I need a few more minutes.

I stare at the veil and I try to will myself into taking the material away.

"I'd like to get a full length mirror for your bedroom, Allyn."

What did he say?

"Huh?" I turn to him in question.

"A mirror. I'd like a full length one for your bedroom. Maybe we can try to find a beautiful old antique at a flea market, or maybe we could have one made specifically for your room. A lovely thick oak frame possibly."

I turn back to the cloth hiding my reflection.

I take a step closer to it.

"Or would you prefer a metal frame? I don't much like metal myself. It's too modern for me. I'd much rather have one with a wooden frame. But it's going in your room, so I think you should choose."

I know what he's doing. He's trying to distract me, to make it easier for me to do this. I fist the edges of the sheet tightly in my hands.

"Or possibly you'd like a mirror without a frame. I could put it directly on your wall, maybe beside the window looking out at the huge tree. You know, I saw a blue jay come and sit on that sill and look inside your room."

The blue jay opens his wings and carelessly flies through the air without a worry in the world. He doesn't look at his body and think how revolting and disgusting he is. He just soars.

Through the elements, through high winds, through rain, hail, or shine, the blue jay glides with such grace.

I yank the cloth off the TV and ball it in my hands. I turn to Dominic, whose smiling eyes are filled with warmth and pride, and I hand him the material. "Could you throw that into the trash, please? I don't need it anymore." And I turn back to face the reflective black surface.

I take a step back and look at the outline of my face.

My vision is blurred, partially because of the damage to my left eye and partially because the screen is a dark black, making it hard to see a perfect representation of myself.

"With pleasure," Dominic says with clear satisfaction as he takes the offensive cloth to the trashcan in the kitchen.

I stare at myself.

Reaching up I touch my face and I can see the woman in the TV screen doing the same thing.

My left eye is droopier than I remember, and my skin is incredibly pasty, so white it almost casts a glow. I remember looking at myself before I was taken, and thinking that I looked pretty. But now, even in the black, I can't see anything that even remotely resembles beauty.

"You're beastly," I murmur to myself as I run my fingers over my lips.

"So gruesome." I touch my left eyelid.

"You're the most incredible woman I've ever met." I turn to see Dominic leaning against the wall with his arms crossed in front of his chest and his legs crossed at the ankle.

"You're blind," I spit back.

"My eyes are wide open and I see beauty that goes far beyond your appearance." He moves off the wall and slowly walks over to the sofa to sit.

I swing back to look at myself again but decide that I don't want to keep looking at the broken woman I see. She makes me too sad.

"Tomorrow, we're going to buy a mirror, and tomorrow night I'm taking you out to that Italian restaurant I was telling you about."

I sit beside Dominic and he wraps his arm around my shoulders. I lean against his strong, masculine frame craving his warmth.

My mind drifts to the blue jay and his unwavering strength as he travels the world.

Predators chase him, but he remains free from harm as he continues to ascend.

If the blue jay can do it, then I can certainly try.

"I'd like an oblong mirror with a solid wooden edge that stands on a frame. Can we have an early dinner, though, because the next day I'd like to go visit my parents and my purple room."

It's time I try to live my life in color.

TWENTY-ONE

"**I**F YOU WANT AN EARLY DINNER, WE NEED TO LEAVE NOW SO WE have enough time to get the furniture store first to find you a mirror," Dominic calls from the front door.

My stomach is in knots and I've locked myself away in the bathroom. The butterflies are fluttering like crazy in my stomach.

"Alright," I call out, not knowing how the hell I'm going to find the courage to leave this bathroom.

"Allyn," Dominic says from the other side of the door. "Can you hear me?"

"Yeah, I can hear you."

"Do you know what I'm looking forward to?" He's trying his signature distraction technique, but right now, it's not working.

I wring my hands together, nervous that I'm going out to be among people for the first time since that day.

"What?"

"I'm ordering the tortellini tonight. Yummo, the Nonna who's the cook, makes it in this rich, creamy, white sauce. It's laden with cheese and butter and bacon and mushrooms. And the tortellini itself is home made. But the thing about her restaurant is you never really know what the house specialty will be until you get there. Everything she makes is so delicious."

"It is?" I call out from inside the bathroom.

"Oh yeah, one time I went there and the only thing she was offering was soup and garlic bread. That was all. And you know what? It was pumpkin soup, something I'd never tried before. Have you ever had pumpkin soup?"

I open the bathroom door and look at Dominic. I can only imagine the perplexed look I must have on my face, because...pumpkin soup? Really? "No, I've never had pumpkin soup before. How was it?"

"It was so damned good, I asked for a second bowl. So I have no idea what we'll get tonight. In a way, I hope it's lasagna, but really, it's whatever she felt like making." He shrugs his shoulders then holds his hand out to me.

"I'm not sure what to have there then."

Holding hands, we walk to the door. The alarm's already off, because I've being leaving the wooden door open with the screen door locked. Dominic unlocks the screen door and pushes it open for me to walk through.

I take a deep breath and step outside onto the porch.

Dominic sets the alarm and taking my keys, locks the house. He stands beside me and wraps his arm around my waist. "Ready?"

I slide my hand into the back pocket of his jeans and we walk to his car, like any normal couple.

"You have to try her iced tea. She makes the best I've ever tasted. But she may not feel like making it today. It really is pot luck with her." He opens the door for me and I easily slide in.

When Dominic's seated beside me in the car, there's a comfortable silence between us. He presses something on the steering wheel and soft music starts to fill the car.

"I can never drive."

"I know." Dominic continues to drive and pay attention to the road.

"If I ever want to go somewhere I'll either have to go by public transport or a cab."

"Or me. I'm happy to take you wherever you want to go."

"But you have to work," I say as I turn my head to look at him.

"No I don't have to, I choose to."

"What does that mean?"

"It means I come from a long line of money, and I've made a lot of my own, too. It means that we can live comfortably for an eternity or longer. It means that you and I won't ever have to worry about money, ever."

"Why are you including me in that statement?" I ask, perplexed by the bizarre words that he just rattled off.

"Because I see you in my future, and if you're with me, you don't need to worry. I'll look after you."

"That's not how this works. I don't need your money, Dominic."

"I'm sorry if I gave you the impression I thought you needed it, because you've done fine on your own financially. I'm saying that I'm going to look after you because I care for you."

I'm momentarily stunned. Clearly, Dominic is serious about his feelings for me. A thought occurs to me as I look out the window and ponder his protective manner.

"Dominic, what have you been doing with the checks that I've been giving you at the end of each week?"

His jaw flexes, and he doesn't answer. I can tell he's hiding the truth from me.

"Dominic?" I question him.

"Um, nothing." His eyes focus on the road and he doesn't look at me.

I press the button on the radio to turn off the background music.

"What do you mean by 'nothing'?" I say, signaling air quotes when I say 'nothing'.

"Exactly what the word implies. I've done nothing with them."

"Have you cashed them?"

Dominic screws his face up a little and shakes his head.

"None of them?" I ask.

"No. Don't get me wrong, at first I forgot to give them to Lauren to take to the bank. And then well, you know," he says coyly.

"No, I don't know, which is why I'm asking you."

"Then we happened. And before we happened, I knew I wanted us to happen, so there was no need for your checks."

"What? That doesn't even make sense."

"It makes sense in my head. It comes down to this… I don't need your money, Allyn. I don't want it. Matter of fact, I want to be the man to look

119

after you and fulfill all your requirements. Regardless of whatever those wants or desires are, I want it to be me who's there for you."

I'm stunned. I don't know what to say to him, so I remain quiet for the rest of the car ride to the furniture store to get my mirror.

Or maybe, it's our mirror.

When we get to the local Art Van Furniture store, Dominic parks the car and gets out to open my door.

But I look around the parking lot, and notice it's fairly busy. There are people coming and going, some carrying bags in their hands, and some with nothing.

"I can't go in there," I say as I point toward the store.

"Why not?"

"There are people everywhere."

I can feel myself begin to shiver and my eyes are darting everywhere, looking around. Scanning. Making sure there's no one suspicious around.

"Yes, there are people everywhere. But the mirrors are inside that store. And unless you've developed telekinetic powers like x-ray vision, then the only way you're going to be able to get the mirror you want for your room is to go in there and buy it. I want you to take my hand and know I'm right beside you. I won't let you fall."

"There are so many people," I whisper to Dominic.

He squats down beside the car and takes my hands in his.

"It doesn't matter where you go, there will always be people everywhere. But remember, I'm right beside you, and I'll move heaven and hell to ensure you're safe. You need to trust in yourself again or you'll never be able to move forward. And I want that beautiful mind as healthy as possible, because we both deserve our own happiness, together."

I gulp down the huge, hard lump sitting in my throat.

Dominic stands and extends his hand down to me.

Trembling, I reach out to touch the warm fingers of the kind, generous man standing before me.

Slowly I slide out of the car and hold onto Dominic like he's my buoy in rough seas.

"You can do this," he says and kisses me on the cheek.

Putting one foot in front of the other and with several stops to slow my racing heart, we finally enter the doors of Art Van Furniture.

My throat begins to constrict, sweat beads on the back of my neck, and I can feel it trickling down my spine. My stomach is in knots and as soon as we're inside, it feels like knives are relentlessly stabbing me in the stomach. My knees start to buckle and I cling to Dominic with both arms tight around his waist.

"I can't do this." A shrill, jittery voice replaces mine.

I'm quaking and shivering and I can barely see straight. I begin to blink rapidly and I feel myself becoming clammy all over as I start to slip into darkness.

"Okay, let's go." Dominic turns us around to head out the door when I see a mirror that I like.

"Wait, I want that mirror." Dominic stops us right in front of it. I can't see my reflection because Dominic is the one the mirror reflects from this angle.

"Do you want us to get it now, or would you prefer I came back to get it tomorrow morning?"

"Can you come back tomorrow please?" I ask. Even though my body's calming, I can't risk staying here any longer.

"Of course." He bends and kisses me softly.

Immediately, I lose my fear with his touch. My shoulders release the tension that held them rigid, and I feel more at ease.

"C'mon, let me take you to dinner," he mumbles against my lips.

His warmth illuminates my darkness, giving me hope that I'll be okay someday.

When we get back in the car, I sit quietly for a few moments and think about my reactions.

"I'm so sorry for what happened back there." I feel like I let Dominic down.

"You have nothing to be sorry for. You did really well. You got out of the car, and even though you recognized the trigger of all the people around, you went inside the store. You even picked out a mirror you like. Really, there's nothing for you to apologize for."

Hmmm. I chew on my lip and let my gaze go to the outside surroundings.

"I suppose I did all those things, didn't I?" And suddenly it occurs to me that I didn't feel that awful, premonitory fear that something bad was about to happen. Maybe I am getting better.

I watch as the sun moves over the hills, quickly disappearing as dusk falls upon us.

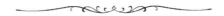

He's right. The restaurant is tiny. There are no more than ten tables inside and another four outside on the incredibly snug terrace.

"Oh, Dominic." The old woman with gray hair piled on top of her head greets us. She grabs his face and kisses him on each cheek.

I smile, watching his face blush as the extravagant old woman pinches his cheeks.

"Who is this bella ma travagliata?" she says, kissing my cheeks before I can make a move to stop her.

"Sorry, what did you say?" I ask.

"I say you very beautiful, but have many troubles," she says in her thick accent. "But you be alright. I see you happy, bella."

Her words take me a little aback and I don't know if I should smile or cry. Am I so broken that it's obvious to everyone?

Or can this old lady see something that only a blessed few can?

"Sedersi, sedersi." She points to a booth at the back of the restaurant.

"She's saying for us to sit down." Dominic translates.

"Do you know Italian?"

"Oh no, but I've been here a lot of times and I understand a few words that she says, like, sit."

We seat opposite each other and the old lady looks on with a huge smile, looking between Dominic and me.

"I make for you insalata e lasagna. You drink chinotto, you like." She walks away without us ordering anything. I'm not entirely sure what just happened.

"See? She's a force of nature. She's bringing us a salad and lasagna and we're drinking chinotto. It's a traditional Italian soda made from oranges. But it's not exactly sweet, it's a little bitter-ish. It's definitely an acquired taste."

"Okay, I'll try it; if I don't like it I'll switch to water."

I look around the restaurant and notice just one other couple sitting inside, holding hands and talking.

"Is it always this quiet?" I ask Dominic.

"Not exactly."

My eyes dart to his, and he looks like the cat that ate the canary. A sheepish look passes over his face as he tries to hold in his smile.

"What aren't you telling me?"

"I sort of anticipated your needs to limit the number of people around. I booked the restaurant for the next two hours, and left just one table inside. All the tables outside are available. This way you can ease back into being around people."

"You did all this for me?"

"Of course."

Oh my.

Everything he's done, he's done for me. Without hesitation and without limits, he's put his life on hold to help me.

I stare into his dynamic brown eyes.

He's perfect.

He's my perfect.

I can hear the rush of my heartbeat thrum intensely in my ears.

This time, I'm not nervous, although I am still petrified of what would happen if I were to step outside into the world alone.

But I am worried of what might happen if I tell him just how much I love him.

TWENTY-TWO

"**A**RE YOU NERVOUS?" I ASK DOMINIC AS HE PACES THE LENGTH of my family room.

"Of course not, don't be preposterous." He scowls at me.

"No? Are you sure about that?" I lean against the back of the sofa as I watch him continue walking back and forth. He stops once and rakes his long fingers through his thick, dark hair and continues his marching.

"To me you look anxious. I've never seen you so agitated and on edge."

"Well I'm not." The fierceness in his voice silences me as he walks over and envelops me in his warm arms. "I'm sorry, it's just I haven't had to meet parents for a very long time. And I wasn't expecting it to be so soon. But I know it's best that it happen now so your parents begin to understand that I'm not going anywhere." He leans in and kisses my mouth. With the softest of touches he sweeps his tongue across my bottom lip and draws it into his mouth, just nibbling tenderly.

"You're forgiven," I say against his lips. "Don't worry about my parents, Dominic. They'll just be pleased we're there. When I called them, they were so happy we're coming to see them. Mom even started crying." My arms stay tight around his waist as Dominic presses a kiss into my hair.

"I'm so proud of your strength, sweetheart." Dominic cradles my face in his hands and allows his thumbs to stroke my cheeks. He leans down and his lips gently meet my own. I feel his body relax as his hands frame my face and his warm moist lips stay glued to mine.

We get lost in the moment, an eternity passing as we revel in the intimacy and closeness of each other's soothing touch.

"We need to go." I sadly break the electric connection between us.

"When I have you in my arms, those are the most perfect moments of my day," Dominic whispers in my ear. "Do you know that?"

A shiver of happiness runs through me. I'm happier than I've felt in a long time.

"Are you ready to go?" Dominic asks as he laces our fingers together and gently tugs me toward the door.

"Yeah I'm ready; let's go." The wooden door was already open and I unlock the screen door, step through and wait for Dominic to lock up so we can head to my parents' home.

"My mom's really looking forward to meeting you. My dad on the other hand…well, he'll be a little harder to convince."

"Your mom's name is Sandra and your dad's is George, right?"

"You remembered." I smile over at Dominic as he pulls out into the street.

Dominic lifts my hand to kiss my knuckles, and a small, nervous smile graces his face.

We drive in silence for the rest of the ten-minute trip. Like the true gentleman that he is, he comes around to open the car door, and holds my hand tightly in his as I rise.

This time, it's me who needs to be his strength.

I can tell that he's got himself in a slight panic. He keeps running his free hand through his hair, then straightens his shirt and his eyes dart around him, taking in his surroundings.

As we walk up the path to my parents' front door, I lean over and say, "Relax. It'll be fine. They know you're important to me, so they'll go easy on you."

A tight, strained smile thins his lips and his nods, acknowledging, but not responding to my words. I squeeze my fingers around his as we take the final few steps to the front door.

I look around the front of the single-level house and notice that not a lot has changed. Though the gardens look a little overrun with weeds, the rest of the façade looks exactly as it did three years ago.

I reach up and press the doorbell and hear a small cry from inside.

Mom flings the door open and without pausing she hauls me in for a hug as tears fall freely down her face.

"I'm so happy, darling. So happy." She keeps repeating, tightening her hold on me until her embrace becomes constricting.

"Mom, you need to let go a little," I say with a giggle.

"I just can't. You're here, you're really here. I'm so happy."

"Step aside, Sandy and let our girl give her old man a hug too," Dad says from behind Mom.

Mom doesn't let me go although she moves to the side and brings Dad into the hug. I'm finally standing on the porch at my parents' house, enfolded in the arms of two people I adore.

"I'm so proud of you," Dad whispers shakily as we continue to hug.

"Come on, let's go inside." Mom breaks the hug and steps to the side to usher us in the door. "Oh I'm so sorry, I'm Sandra and you must be Dominic." Mom extends her hand to Dominic and he gently takes it in his and shakes it.

"Ma'am, it's a pleasure to meet you."

"Oh please, it's just Sandra. Please come inside."

Dad doesn't let me go. He continues to hold me close to his chest. I can feel his shoulders shaking and I can hear the sniffling coming as he gulps for air. "This is all I wanted, for you to be able to leave your home."

"I know, Dad. And I've finally done it. All thanks to Dominic," I breathe as I continue to hug my father.

"Come on, let's go inside and talk." Dad's hand holds mine as we step inside the house.

Everything inside looks exactly the same too. Not a single thing has changed.

"Here, sit." Dad points to the sofa.

Dominic sits in the lone armchair and I sit nestled between Mom and Dad.

"Oh, who'd like a coffee?" Mom asks.

"I'd just like some water, Sandra, please," Dominic answers.

"Me too, Mom."

Mom goes toward the kitchen, leaving my dad, me, and Dominic. Dad looks over toward Dominic and I watch as he eyes Dominic before furrowing his eyebrows together.

"How old are you, Dominic?"

"I'm thirty-eight, Sir."

"Hmmm," Dad scowls at Dominic.

"Dad," I whisper. "Don't, please."

Mom comes back in with a huge smile and four glasses of iced water as I watch Dad and Dominic have a silent conversation.

Dad stands the moment Mom sits and rubs his hands down his jean-clad thighs.

"A word, please, Dominic," he says as he heads toward the back door, not looking back to see if Dominic follows.

"I'll go too," I say as I stand and move to go outside.

Dominic places a hand around my upper arm and pulls me back. He moves so he's standing in front of me, in order for me to see him better.

"There's no need to come. Your father and I have a few things to discuss. Stay here and talk with your mom," he says in a low voice. With a smile, he adds, "Go see if your room is still four shades of purple."

"Dominic, I think I should come with you," I say, frustrated that he's trying to stop me.

"Sweetheart," he starts as he rubs his hands up and down my arms, causing goose bumps to form from the simple exchange. "I'll be fine." He leans down and chastely kisses my lips before letting go of my arms. He presses another kiss to my forehead and follows Dad outside.

Dominic

"You're thirty-eight?" Allyn's father says, starting this rather awkward conversation.

"Yes, sir I am. I'll be turning thirty-nine in about three weeks."

George paces along the back porch and stops to look me over then continues his marching.

"And you're her doctor too."

"Yes, sir I'm that as well."

George takes a few steps toward me and I straighten my back to show that I'm not intimidated by his protective nature toward his daughter.

"Doesn't that cause an issue for your doctor-patient relationship? Isn't there a code of ethics you should be upholding?" He crosses his arms in front of him and plants his feet hip-width apart. I can tell he's not entirely pleased with the idea of Allyn and me together.

"Technically, yes. But I can't help who I've fallen for, sir. She's an amazing woman."

"She's survived a lot. I don't want her to have to survive you too. You're considerably older than Allyn, and when you decide that she's too young for you and dump her, she'll be back where she started, if not worse."

"I understand your concern, but that's not going to happen. Allyn is wise beyond her years, and she's perfect just the way she is."

George takes a step closer to me.

"You're aware that she'll never work again? She'll never be able to go out on her own, and she'll be living in fear the rest of her life?"

"Sir, with all due respect, but I think Allyn is much stronger than you think and she will certainly be able to do everything you've just listed and much more."

"She can't give you children."

"I know all about what those monsters did to her."

"Why is a thirty-eight year old man, who seems quite intelligent, financially secure and handsome, not married with his own family?"

Oh shit. I'm going to have to tell him something about Chelsea.

"Truthfully, I am married." I see George's face turn ashen as his hands ball up into fists. "I'm waiting for my divorce to come through any day now. My brother is my lawyer and he worked hard to fast-track it, but I still need to wait for it to be finalized, and even he can't hurry that up."

George retreats one step, and unclasps his hands. He turns to look out on the small, lively garden and leans up against the railing while he takes in a huge gulp of air.

"Sir, may I be honest with you?" I take a step closer and mimic his position and posture.

"Of course."

"Allyn is the most important person in my life. I can't even think about not being with her. I'll protect her, I'll nurture her, and I'll help her heal. I know I'll never find anyone who touches my heart as deeply as Allyn does."

"But her scars...," her father starts.

"Are inconsequential. I don't even see them; I never have," I respond.

"But the age difference..."

"Will only matter to the haters. And unfortunately, they're everywhere. I pay them no due, because their opinion means nothing to me. Only Allyn's opinion matters. If she'll let me, I'll stay with her until the very last breath I take."

A prolonged silence passes between us. George must be considering what I've said. The intensity of the moment makes the pounding of my heart reverberate loudly in my ears, as I allow the father of the woman I love to digest my honest words.

"Do you know what, Dominic?" He waits for me to respond.

"No Sir, what?"

"I think you'd best call me George."

TWENTY-THREE

"*G*UESS WHAT?" DOMINIC SAYS AS HE GETS OFF THE PHONE WITH his brother.

"What?"

"I've got two things to tell you, actually. First, the mirror will be delivered this afternoon." He looks at the clock that hangs over TV, and then looks back at me. "It'll be here in about an hour."

Shit. I stiffen and feel the fear slowly creep into me, and a wave of nausea grips my stomach.

"Okay, that's good. I guess." I'm not fooling Dominic. He knows how stressed I am.

"And a second thing just happened." He stops talking and in four large strides embraces me in a huge bear hug. "My divorce has been finalized," he murmurs as he kisses my forehead.

"I'm really happy for you, Dominic." I nuzzle closer into him, trying to draw strength from the intimacy between us.

Dominic's body vibrates with elation and I can feel his good mood penetrating straight through to my soul. Things are looking up for us. I'm getting a mirror in here, and his divorce is finally settled.

Despite my momentary fear, I can't help but feel jubilation at everything that's happening for us. And for me.

Two short months ago I slept with a knife under my pillow, and couldn't go further than three steps without checking for my panic button. I was absolutely enshrouded by a massive cloud of terror and fear.

Today, that knife is in a drawer in the kitchen. The panic button has been retired to the hallway table, and I even leave the wooden door open to let fresh air into my home.

Standing in Dominic's embrace, I can't help but think that all of this has been made possible only by the amazing efforts of the man I love.

"Dominic?"

"Hmmm," he murmurs as his hands softly trail up and down on either side of my spine.

"I love you," I whisper in the tiniest of voices. A burn flashes through me as I realize what I've admitted.

Dominic's hands stop the sensual movements on my back. He moves away slightly so he can kiss my nose then leans down so our foreheads are touching.

"Say it again," he demands, "but you need to say it louder."

"I love you." My stomach is still churning and I don't know if this moment was the right time for me to tell him. But I don't care. I've been through so much shit in my life that I need him to know how I feel. He's the one for me, and I don't give a damn about the timing.

He cups my face and tips it up so I look into his mesmerizing, blazing orbs.

"My heart is yours. My soul belongs to you because I love you with everything that I am," he whispers.

The affection in my heart increases with every word that passes Dominic's lips, and tears fall freely from my eyes.

He loves me.

"Are those happy tears?" Dominic wipes my cheeks with the pad of his thumbs. "Even crying, you're still the most beautiful woman I've ever met."

My emotions heighten with every morsel of sound that Dominic says.

"Sweetheart?" I look up at Dominic and his eyes narrow with concern, most likely because I haven't been able to speak yet.

A smile dances on my lips as I gather the right words for Dominic. But

I don't know what those words should be. "Thank you for loving me. I didn't think anyone ever would again."

The edges of his mouth lift and his eyes soften. His hands rest at the small of my back.

"I love you," Dominic affirms.

We stand together, quite content to simply share this embrace.

Before long, there's a knock at the front door and we both know that it's the delivery of the mirror.

I instantly stiffen and instinctively resist allowing anyone into my home. Dominic must sense my trepidation, holding me closer to him.

"Do you want to wait in the kitchen?" he asks.

I just nod my head without saying a word.

"Okay, how about you make us each a coffee then? I'll be back in a moment, as soon as they leave."

My heart's beating so rapidly that I feel like I'm heading straight into a panic attack.

You can do this, Allyn.

I walk into the kitchen and flick the switch on my coffee machine. I wait for the light to turn green, indicating that it's ready to be used. But all I can think about are the stranger's footsteps I hear on the stairs.

"'Scuse me, lady. Gotta bathroom I can use, please?"

I whirl around to see a burly older man in a blue uniform standing at the entrance to the kitchen.

My heart stops.

My breath hitches.

Black spots dance in front of my eyes.

My entire body is covered in goose bumps.

My stomach roils and knots.

"You alright, love? You don't look so good," the burly man says and takes a step toward me, his hand out.

My eyes fall to his feet as he takes another step closer.

I feel myself shaking and shivering and my mouth falls open as I gasp for air.

I grab the edge of the counter and my legs suddenly refuse to hold me. I crumple to the floor.

"Get out! Get out now!" I hear Dominic yelling at the man.

"I didn't do nothing, I'm sorry, I'm so sorry," the burly man sputters as he holds both hands up in surrender and backs out of the kitchen.

"Get out!" Dominic's still yelling at the man.

"I'm sorry, lady," the man says again and turns to leave.

I hear the front door shut and quick heavy footsteps as Dominic runs back to me after locking the door.

"They're gone. I'm sorry. One carried the mirror upstairs and I didn't see the other one. I'm so sorry, Allyn." He helps me up from the floor and holds me tight to his body.

"A-alarm," I try to verbalize but the sound is more like an inaudible mumble.

"What do you need?"

"Alarm, put it on," I plead as I look up at Dominic. It takes a moment for him to understand my meaning.

He lets me go and takes the few steps to the keypad and punches in my code, immediately returning to hold me.

"Come on. Let's go lie down." He carefully leads me upstairs and I follow him.

When we reach my bedroom, I see the mirror standing tall in the corner, but the mirror part is covered in beige paper so I can't see my reflection.

Dominic pulls the covers back and sits me down on the bed. I lie back and he leans down to take my shoes off, and then slips in beside me.

He reaches his arm out and I shape my body into his. His hand slides over my hair as I listen to the steady beat of his heart. Dominic breathes in and exhales. I count his breaths and synchronize my breathing with his. As his breathing begins to calm, I begin to release the anxiety I'm holding on to so tightly.

"What happened?" he asks calmly.

I shut my eyes and close the tiny gap between our bodies, molding myself against him. Becoming one with Dominic.

"He asked to use the bathroom," I say as my face burns from the embarrassment of melting down over something as stupid as that.

"Anything else?"

"No nothing else. He was very nice; he asked me if I was alright. But the moment he stepped toward me, my entire body shut down and my brain was frozen in fear."

Again we're surrounded by silence and I notice a change in Dominic's breathing. It's becoming more rapid, forcing my body to comply with the same rhythm.

"You didn't tell me what happened with my Dad yesterday."

"We understand each other now. He was worried that I would end up hurting you, but we hashed out a few things and he now knows that I'm not going anywhere."

I move and put my leg over Dominic's thigh.

Dominic tries to hold in a growl, but I feel it reverberate through his chest and it makes me giggle.

"I noticed that you were calling Dad by his first name when you both came back inside. That's a pretty big deal for Dad. He usually only allows people to call him Sir or Mr. Sommers, so you must've done something right."

"He did ask me why I wasn't married with children." My body stiffens, knowing that children are something that Dominic wants that I can't give him. "And I told him that my divorce was close, but I didn't tell him why. It's not his business; it's only mine, Chelsea's, and now yours."

That word keeps getting to me. Children.

"How much does it affect you that I can't give you what you want?"

"In reference to what?"

"Children."

"Allyn, sit up please."

We both sit up in bed and stare into each other's eyes. I can't look away from him. He looks so angry or maybe he's upset.

"I love you more than I've ever loved anyone in my life. If I knew you existed in the universe, I would have been searching for you a long time ago. Yes, I'd love to have a child, and a baby with you would be absolutely perfect. But I'd rather know you love me than have a house filled with children."

"I'm sorry I can't give you both," I say as I cast my gaze downward and nervously play with the hem of my t-shirt.

"You've given me your heart, and that's more than I ever hoped for."

His mouth engulfs mine and he rubs his palms down my bare arm, encouraging me to relax and stop dwelling on the negative.

Dominic's tongue slowly emerges, cautiously exploring my upper lip before he changes it to a closed-mouth kiss.

Longingly, I lean forward trying to join his lips to mine again. I'm rewarded as he pulls me to him for a scorching kiss. I move my hands to tangle in his hair and grasp at the back of his head while moving my body to straddle his lap.

"Oh God," Dominic rasps against my mouth.

I brush my lips against Dominic's warm mouth, tasting him and allowing myself to boldly explore him. Worshipping the natural line of his mouth with my tongue, I stop and nibble at his bottom lip before continuing to move across his skin.

"You need to stop, Allyn." He grips my hips tightly and holds me in place, contradicting his words.

Dominic lolls his head back and his neck is completely exposed to me. There's a light cover of stubble across his throat and his Adam's apple moves as he struggles to swallow.

I slowly ghost my fingertips along his jawline to his chin. Dominic's breath becomes rapid and his fingers tighten even more on my hips.

I follow the perfect line from his chin, down his neck to the top of his t-shirt. With a hand on Dominic's chest I move over his sternum and rest it over his heart.

"Allyn, your touch is heaven. But I need for you to stop, please, right now." He lets go of my hips and moves me off his lap.

I turn over and lie down with my back to Dominic and curl up into myself, embarrassed that when I tried taking it further, he rejected me.

"Sweetheart, there's a fever burning deep inside me and I want you so badly." He turns behind me and places a hand on my hip, but no other part of his body is touching me. "But when we do make love, I want it to be because we want to enjoy each other's body and soul. I don't want it to be a coping mechanism every time either of us faces a trigger."

Is that what I was doing?

I almost had a panic attack, and ended up trying to take our relationship to its ultimate level.

Fuck, he's right. I was trying to use making love to Dominic to overcome a difficult situation.

"I understand," I sigh as I turn to look into Dominic's face.

"I knew you would." He gets off the bed and stands with his hand extended to me. I feel my eyebrows knit together, silently questioning his offered hand. "Let's go downstairs and make dinner. And when you're ready, we'll uncover that mirror."

"Not today," I say as I look over at the covered mirror. "But one day very soon."

Soon, I'll draw on all my strength to look at myself, and I hope I can keep from hating the ugly part of me.

TWENTY-FOUR

"**S**WEETHEART, FOR THE LAST TEN DAYS YOU'VE BEEN COMING up here, sitting on the bed and just staring at the mirror. Do you think it may be time to take the paper off it and move it over to stand next to the window?" Dominic says from behind me as I continue to stare at it, as if it's malignant and needs to be removed before the illness can spread.

"I'm still not sure," I sigh and turn my head to look at Dominic standing in the doorway.

"The longer you leave it, the more difficult the situation will become. You've come so far already, Allyn. I think it's best if you remove the paper and face your reflection. It will show you the most amazing woman I've ever known." His face sports a wide, encouraging smile.

"What if I don't like what I see?"

"Then we'll have to work on it. I want you to do more than like your reflection, I want you to love it."

I turn back to look at the innocent piece of glass and wood, and I can imagine seeing myself in it.

This is something that I need to do, and it's ripping me apart that it's so hard to face myself. I've built up the dread of seeing my sickening, repulsive body to such a degree that now I'm at a loss as to how to reconnect with myself.

"We'll do it together, after dinner." I turn back around and silently steel myself to do it.

"Great, because dinner's done," Dominic says happily. "Come on, I'm just about to serve." He heads downstairs, leaving me to scowl at the mirror and blame it for my confused emotions.

"Damn it," I yell at the mirror.

Stupid mirror, standing in the corner, taunting me, daring to me to unveil it and to finally look at myself.

Stupid mirror.

Stupid me.

"Allyn," Dominic shouts from downstairs.

"Coming." I keep staring at the mirror while I stand slowly from my bed, my eyes focused on the damn thing. A small wave of courage begins to wash over me.

I can do this.

I've overcome so much, and this is just another hurdle for me to tackle.

Screw it.

A meager obstacle.

I straighten my back and turn away from it, letting it cause no further disruption to my life. I won't let it rule me.

Ten days I've watched it with dread, and finally I've found my peace with it.

I'm excited as I walk down the stairs with a spring in my step, going to Dominic. He's standing in front of the stove, wearing oven mitts, taking a dish out of the oven.

I go straight to him, and when he places the dish on the kitchen counter, I don't think twice about taking his mouth in a kiss.

"After our meal, that beige paper is garbage." I say before returning to our kiss. "Can I help with dinner?"

"Already done, you just need to sit and enjoy." Dominic juts his chin for me to go sit at the kitchen table.

"What are we having?"

"Pot roast, and homemade lemonade."

Instantly I'm reminded of his last attempt at lemonade, and it must show on my face because he stares at me with a bemused look. "I remembered the sugar this time. You don't need to screw your nose up like that," he teases, chuckling.

I giggle at his playfulness. Dominic places a bowl in front of me and takes a carafe of lemonade out of the fridge. He carefully pours tall glasses for both of us.

"Thank you," I say. "This all looks delicious." I bring the glass to my lips and take a small sip of lemonade. "It's zesty and flavorful, with just the right amount of sugar."

Dominic expels a huge breath and smiles as he tastes his lemonade. "Ummm, it really is quite good," he says admiring his own work.

Dominic sits down and we both start dinner in happy, high spirits.

"Are you ready to meet my family on Sunday?"

"I am, actually. But I'm more excited to share your birthday with you."

"Ugh, don't remind me of that." He smiles at me merrily and takes another bite of his dinner.

"Hmmm, thirty-nine, what can I possibly give you?"

"There's nothing that I want but you."

A small grin curls my mouth, but I remain quiet as we continue with our tasty dinner.

"It's time to take the paper off," Dominic urges quietly as I stand in front of the mirror. He's standing behind me.

With shaky hands, I peel off the little bit of tape at the top right corner that's securing the beige paper to the wooden frame.

My breathing is accelerated and those pesky butterflies are fluttering around inside my stomach, trying to burst through.

I can feel myself chewing on the inside of my cheek as I argue with myself about removing the paper.

Throwing it away once and for all.

Removing the beige from my life.

Dominic slides his hand onto my hip.

"Do you know just how beautiful you are?"

"I'm scarred, Dominic."

"I love your smile." He drags his mouth across the junction of my shoulder and neck.

"My lips are thin."

"I adore your expressive, stormy eyes." He moves his mouth a little further up my neck.

"My left eye droops and I can't see properly out of it."

Dominic's hand moves around to my abdomen and he spreads his fingers wide as he pulls me against his powerful chest.

"Every time you kiss me, I know I've been blessed." His lips linger just below my ear, not touching me. His warm breath is like an electrical current, zapping my skin and causing instant embers of lust to glow with intensity.

"I'm seeing more and more color because of you," I sigh as my head rests against Dominic's chest.

"Rip away the beige and look at the perfect woman who stands before me."

I open my eyes and reach up to the tape. Without hesitation I rip it in one fluid down motion, taking a third of the paper off.

I catch a glimpse of the broken girl doing the same thing I am. I stop momentarily to look at her.

"Don't stop, Allyn, tear the rest of it off," Dominic encourages me.

I close my eyes, take a deep breath, and with Dominic standing behind me, snap my eyes open and shred the fucking beige.

Dominic moves the paper out of the way. I stand in front of the mirror, studying the pale, sad girl looking back at me.

Everything else in the room dissolves into nothingness as I look at the girl with strawberry blonde hair.

It feels like my heart stops beating. The blood in my veins turns icy.

"I didn't realize just how vile I actually am." I reach up to touch my lips as I look at the reflection of my broken eye.

"I see beauty there." Dominic's hand snakes around to rest over my heart. "And courage here." He pets my hair with his free hand. "Strength radiates off you, Allyn." His lips meet my cheek and I continue to stare at me.

"I've not seen myself properly for so many years that now I'm appalled by how I look."

"You see a woman scarred, I see the woman I love."

I turn my head to look at Dominic. "How can you say you love me? I'm nowhere near attractive."

"Because your body might be scarred, your soul may be broken, but I see the brilliant light that comes from deep inside you. Don't you see it? It's not about me loving you, but about you loving me. You've brought me back to life, Allyn. You've given me breath when I thought I was never going to find that spark again. And I found it, with you."

I turn my body so I'm facing Dominic.

He shakes his head and gently turns me back around.

"You need to face yourself, Allyn. You need to see the amazing woman that I see."

Dominic steps out of the reflection. Maybe he's gone downstairs; maybe he's waiting in the hall outside my bedroom. I don't know. All I know is I'm alone now with my reflection.

My eyes find my reflection again in the mirror. The monsters in my head laugh at me. They're telling me how ugly I am.

They yell at me, screaming in their angriest voices just how vulgar and disgusting I am. Telling me how they see me, how the world perceives me. How I look at myself.

My shoulders are slumped down and my head is slightly lowered. I look defeated, with no pride in myself. My face is so, worn. So used and crushed, with my droopy eye and the scars that my eyes automatically draw to. I lift my hair and tilt my head looking at where the top of my right ear has been bitten off.

I look mutilated.

"You're shockingly marked," they shout at me. "No one could want you," they taunt me. "Your body is ugly. Look at your throat."

I tilt my head and look at the knife mark that runs along my throat. I lift my hand and slowly run my fingertips down the length of the scar. The angry, red mark feels bumpy from start to finish, but it's so soft.

"Why are you so mad at me?" I ask the woman looking at me, talking to the monsters she's brought with her. "I didn't choose this. I didn't ask to be taken, or knifed, or raped. So why do you look at me with so much hate?"

The woman says nothing in return. I hear the monsters chuckle.

"Why are you so angry? You can't look at me without hellfire burning from your eyes. They did this; they took me and hurt me. I didn't volunteer to be brutalized and debased, they did it." I point out the door.

"It's not on me!" I yell as my hand beats against my chest. "It's on them!" I scream at the woman in the mirror. "Don't hate me because of what they did to me."

But the eyes of the woman looking back at me are filled with pity behind the anger.

"They did it. Not me," I whisper to her. A tear rolls down her face and she swipes at it with her fingertips, but her sad eyes remain glued to mine.

I know she's trying to tell me something, but I can't understand her yet.

"Tell me," I say as sit on the floor. The woman in the mirror does, too.

"I need to know why you hate me so much."

She continues to gaze at me with the sorrow that covers her entire being. It breaks my heart.

"Please, I need to understand why you resent me so. Have I taken something for granted and not realized it? Have I betrayed you in some way?"

She doesn't falter; she doesn't move. She simply looks utterly lost.

I bury my face into my hands and try to breathe through the pain.

I look back at the woman and bring my legs up to hug my knees. She copies me, wrapping her arms around her legs, too. I lean my chin onto my knees and stare at my fragmented doppelganger.

"My life isn't worth living if you can't explain why you hold so much venom toward me. I need to know why, in order to go on." I look away from her tortured eyes.

"I do resent you," she responds in a quiet, almost inaudible voice.

My eyes fly to hers and we're locked in a staring match.

"Why do you resent me?" I ask with sheer desperation soaking my voice. But she continues to look at me with nothing more than the same grief she's held ever since the paper came off the mirror.

She remains quiet.

I close my eyes and let my head rest onto my knees.

"I resent you because you choose to stay broken," she says a little louder. I don't dare lift my head or she'll stop talking again. "You fought so hard to stay alive when it happened, but now you fight equally hard not to live. And I resent you for stopping us from living."

Is that what I'm doing?

Not living?

I lift my head and see her staring hopefully at me. She's made her very valid point and it's forced me to re-evaluate myself.

"You want me to forget what they did? To pretend it didn't happen? To act as if it won't happen again?" I ask her. But she's quiet. "I can't forget. I'll never be able to." I look out the window and see the blue jay sitting on the window sill.

"No, don't forget. Don't pretend. Just start living. For you, for me, and for all those who love you," she whispers quietly.

At that very moment, the blue jay spreads his wings and takes a leap of faith, confident his wings will carry him.

"Allyn," Dominic gently calls to me.

I stand and turn to look at him. For the first time in three years, I feel almost free.

"Are you alright? You've been in here for over an hour."

Without concern, I run into his arms and snuggle against his chest as he holds me close in his warmth.

"I'm better than alright," I say as I smile against his chest.

I open my mind, and resolve that I too will take a leap of faith and let my wings carry me to freedom.

TWENTY-FIVE

*D*OMINIC AND I SIT ON THE SOFA AS HE FLICKS THROUGH THE channels looking for a movie that we both want to watch.

He stops on a wrestling tournament and I roll my eyes. What is with men and wrestling?

Looking away, I try to hide my scorn, but when Dominic turns his head I fake a yawn and look away.

"Is this boring you?" he asks.

"Hmmm, looks like you may be the new Sherlock Holmes," I tease with a smile.

"Did you just huff at me?" He moves a little closer to me on the lounge.

"Not entirely, what I did was roll my eyes at you and yawn, not huff. Two entirely different things, Dr. Shriver."

I chance a look at him and he's gaping at me with an eyebrow lifted, though he definitely sees the humor because the corners of his lips are lifted.

"And you just called me Dr. Shriver, I thought I told you that it makes me sound like a pompous old ass."

"Well you are turning thirty-nine in three days' time. All I'm saying is that if the title fits..." I look away trying my hardest to conceal the giggle that's bursting to escape.

Dominic scoots over so he's now sitting way too close to me. There's a menacing twinkle in his eyes. I have a feeling tumbling around deep inside of me that he's about to tickle me.

With snake-like speed his hand darts out, wraps it around my upper arm and pulls me to him. There's only one spot I'm ticklish, and that's the soles of my feet. If I can keep them firmly planted on the ground, there's no way he'll be able to figure it out.

He digs his fingers into my waist and tries to tickle me.

"Really? You think I'm ticklish?" I try to deny the truth, praying that he doesn't go for my feet.

"Aren't you? You've gotta be ticklish under your arms."

I lift my arms over my head and give him a daring look.

"Huh, under your chin?" he asks as he tries tickling me there.

I giggle to try and throw him off track, but his eyes narrow and a huge grin lights up his face.

Oh no, I think I'm in trouble.

He grabs my calf and lifts my foot in one smooth action and starts tickling the sole of my foot with feather-light touches.

I'm wriggling maniacally on the sofa, trying my hardest to get away from him, but at the same time I'm laughing so hard that I can't catch my breath.

"St..." I try and tell him to stop but he's now got both my feet in his one big hand and is concentrating on tickling them.

"St..." I breathe between gales of laughter.

Dominic's kneeling on the floor in front of me and leans down. He bites the edge of my foot, not hard, but with enough pressure to cause me to gulp and instantly stop laughing.

Dominic looks up at me and his fun, carefree nature is now gone, replaced by a heated blaze deep within his eyes.

He brings my foot to his face and kisses the arch, then does the same with my other foot.

A warm turbulence starts building within me, a need that I've not felt for three years.

Dominic slides his hands up my calves with pleasing pressure. He tightens his grip like he's giving me a massage. His mouth skims up my left leg, just giving me small, arousing nips from my ankle to my knee.

He stops at the knee and nibbles softly, laving me with his wet, raspy tongue before taking skin in his mouth and gently pulling it between his teeth.

I close my eyes, rest my head on the giant, fluffy pillow behind me, and allow myself to feel how beautiful this moment is.

Dominic moves his mouth and his hands to mid-thigh and slowly inches a little further up.

My body stiffens beneath his touch and Dominic moves his mouth away from me but keeps his hands on my thighs.

"Nothing has to happen," he reassures me with his words.

I sit up so I can see him, and give him a small, wan smile. "I want to try, but I'm not sure how far I'll be able to take this. I don't want to disappoint you again."

"We'll only go as far as you're comfortable. Tell me to stop, and I will," he says as he continues to stare into my eyes and stroke my thighs.

I'm captivated by his stunning face, his square jawline, his slightly crooked nose, and his deep, dark brown eyes, I want this. I want to accept his body and complete our union.

But I can't push myself to a point where I'll revert to the recluse I was a few short months ago.

Still, I want to try.

Dominic's relentless mouth slowly lowers to my thigh. I watch him lay kiss upon kiss on me as he slowly moves up my leg. My legs spread wider to accommodate his body and he pushes my skirt to the top of my thighs.

"Is this okay, sweetheart?" There's an ardent undertone in his voice, and scorching heat is emanating from his hands as they gently creep toward my covered sex.

"Yes," I sigh, struggling to breathe through a salacious need.

His fingers gently stroke me through my panties. My body tightens, then relaxes as I continue to stare in Dominic's eyes. He slides his hand under the material and carefully inserts a finger into me, testing me to make sure I'm alright with this, giving me time to adjust.

Not once does he look away from my eyes, and his searing gaze holds me connected to him. He twirls the finger inside me and slowly adds a second, stretching me as he moves them in and out slowly, then more quickly. He scissors his fingers and the action causes me to wince, but the pain lasts for no more than a few seconds before it morphs into pleasure, overtaking my entire body.

Hunger rises from deep within me, and my hips start rolling as Dominic continues to move his fingers in and out, up then down, deep inside then right to the edge of my sex. His thumb moves to circle over my clit, and suddenly, I'm right on the edge.

My breath becomes labored and my eyes close so I can concentrate on this exquisite, bubbling feeling that's taking my body hostage.

Without warning, Dominic speeds up and my body flings off the sofa as a harsh cry of pleasure rips from my throat.

My heart's racing as unparalleled satisfaction soaks into of every part of my body.

Dominic's mouth silences my gasping breath as he sits beside me and pulls me to lean against him.

"Thank you," I whisper as I move to straddle his legs. I reach down and pull his t-shirt over his head, not able to keep my hands from stroking his tight chest.

His arousal is pressing against my sex and I move my hips a little to get more of him near me. Despite having just climaxed, the friction is tantalizing. I move my hands to the button on his trousers.

"You don't have to," he says as he covers my hands with his, stilling my movement.

"I want to. I want to try and give you pleasure."

He exhales a huge breath and nods just slightly as he removes his hand. I move off him, and he takes his trousers and boxers off in one movement.

Wow, he's beautiful to look at. Everywhere.

I tenderly wrap my hand around his shaft, but my fingers don't close around his girth. I slide my hand up to the tip of his cock and just trace the slit with my index finger.

An unrecognizable groan bursts past Dominic's mouth. "Grip me a little harder," he says as he tightens his fingers around mine to show me the pressure that he likes.

Moving up and down the length of him, I maintain the grip he showed me. "Am I doing okay? I've only ever done this once before. I'm sorry if

I'm doing it wrong."

"Sweetheart, your touch is so wonderful. Grab my balls with your other hand and squeeze them gently as you pull."

I watch his face to make sure I'm not hurting him, but he doesn't look like he's in pain. Well, not any sort of bad pain.

"A little quicker on the strokes, and a little harder as you pull my balls," he rasps breathing heavily.

I follow his commands and watch as his face is overtaken with pleasure. I know that feeling. He gave it to me only a little while ago.

"I need you to kiss me, but don't stop what you're doing with your hands." His jaw is tense and tight and he slightly bucks up into my hand. Leaning over, I kiss him.

And kiss him.

And damn well keep kissing him.

His touch is fevered. His fingers are laced tightly in my hair, holding my lips to his. His hips buck strongly in my hands.

With my mouth dancing over his and our hearts beating wildly we find the perfect rhythm to continue our ballet.

"Infinity," Dominic mumbles against my lips, his breathing heavy. "That's how much I love you."

Dominic lets out a low moan and I feel warm, sticky fluid hit my hand.

"I'm so sorry," he says as I pull away from his kiss to look down between us at the milky white substance covering my hand and his stomach.

I suppress a smile so he doesn't feel bad. "It's alright."

He jumps up and gives me his t-shirt, "Here, wipe it off with this," he says, looking quite embarrassed.

"Don't be silly." I get up off the sofa and go to the bathroom to wash my hands.

When I get back, Dominic's dressed and sitting in the family room with the TV turned off, looking quite contrite.

"Did I do something wrong?" I ask. "Because I can do better; you just have to teach me."

He takes my hands in his, lifts them and kisses all my fingers. "No, you were wonderful. I just hope I didn't push you too far."

"I wanted to try that, to give you pleasure. But I don't think I'm ready to do more yet."

Damn it, why do I feel like I'm denying his most basic need? I frown, feeling like a failure.

"Hey, why are you sad?" he asks as he runs his hand through my hair, separating the strands between his fingers.

"Because I can't give you what you need yet. I'm so sorry. I mean I'll understand if you want to…" I trail off because even though I can't bear the thought of him turning to another woman, even if I do understand that as a man, he has certain desires.

He lifts my chin with a crooked finger and stares into my eyes. "What do you take me for? There's only one woman I want and she's sitting here beside me. I've never given you any reason to doubt me, or my feelings for you, have I? Please dismiss those negative thoughts from your beautiful mind. I only want you." He kisses me. "Just." Kiss. "You." Kiss, kiss.

"I'm sorry."

"Stop apologizing. What we just did was love in its most absolute form. So please, never say you're sorry for anything we share together. Regardless of whether it's inside or outside the bedroom."

I smile when I hear his words.

We mold our bodies together as he turns the TV on and we watch a re-run of Hogan's Heroes.

My mind begins to drift, as I look around my beige family room. My feet are curled up on my beige sofa, and Dominic's arm is resting on a beige pillow.

"Dominic."

"Hmmm." He chuckles at the episode on TV.

"I think I'd like a purple family room." I look around and imagine the exact hue I want, splattered artfully on my walls.

"I'll hire a female painter," he says as he kisses the top of my head.

I smile and close my eyes.

This blue jay has spread her wings.

TWENTY-SIX

"HOW FAR AWAY DO YOUR PARENTS LIVE?" I ASK AS DOMINIC navigates the roads.

"A little under half an hour. My brother is about another fifteen minutes away from there."

He holds my hand on his thigh as he drives. I look out my window and take in the magnificence of nature.

It's almost the end of summer and even though the days still hold heat in the air, the nights have become a little chilly. This afternoon there are a few gray clouds hanging around, but they appear to be distant and aren't really going to bother us.

"You look beautiful tonight, Allyn."

I look down at my long, calf-length black skirt and my pale yellow blouse and make a note that I want to add other colors to my wardrobe. Brighter, happier hues to reflect the brighter and happier me.

We get to an exclusive, gated community and Dominic pulls up alongside the guard house. The guard smiles and opens the gates for Dominic without saying a word to him.

I look over at Dominic in question. He glances at me and smiles. "That's Phil. He's been here for more years than I care to remember. He's a good guy, too."

The houses in this estate are nothing less than breathtaking and opulent, regal and stunning. Large Victorian-style mansions sprawl out on generous acreage.

Dominic drives slowly through the wide, tree-lined streets. He comes to a stop in front of a home that rivals the most majestic here. The sun is setting but there's still enough light to see the homes scattered with artful precision. A sleek, blue convertible sports car sits proudly in the driveway, and I smile at the fact that Dominic's father and mother would go zipping around in a car like that.

I haven't met them yet. Dominic describes them as being proper and refined, so imagining them speeding down the interstate with the roof down and the wind blowing through their hair causes me to giggle.

"What's funny?" Dominic asks as he opens his door before coming around and opening mine.

"Your parents' sports car." I point to the sculptured vehicle.

"Well that is funny, because that's not their car. They each own the latest model Range Rover, not something like that. It must be Oscar's, hmmm...strange he didn't mention buying a new car." Dominic scowls and the grip he has around my hand tightens. "I wonder what sort of skank he brought home with him tonight," he murmurs, more to himself then to me.

We walk the long drive way and I begin to get nervous.

"Why are you trembling?" Dominic asks and puts his arm around my waist.

"What if they don't like me?" I anxiously tug at the bottom of my blouse, wishing I'd worn something a little more sophisticated.

"They won't like you, sweetheart. They'll love you, just like I do. You make me happy and they'll be over the moon that we've found each other."

When Dominic and I reach the front door, he turns the knob and we step through. He's pulling me along, but my body is screaming apprehension, and my mind is struggling with entering surroundings that I have no control over. I come to a sudden halt.

At home I know where everything is, where my panic buttons are, and where I can hide. I don't know this place.

"Allyn, look at me."

I look up and Dominic's eyes regarding me with concern, but there's a softness to his features too.

"Hold my hand and don't let go. Take a deep breath, Allyn."

I breathe in and hold it, but continue to stare into Dominic's dark brown orbs.

"One, two, three," his voice lowers. "Four, breathe out, five, six, seven."

I take another deep breath and my lips turn up in a small smile.

"I'm alright. I'll be fine. Thank you," I whisper.

Dominic leans down, kisses me softly and tenderly runs his knuckles down the length of my jaw.

"Are you ready to meet my family now?" he asks as his lips hover over mine.

I just nod and stretch my neck to receive another kiss.

"Mom, Dad we're here," Dominic calls out.

"In the family room," they respond.

"Come on, back here," Dominic coaxes, not releasing my hand. We walk past a grand staircase that leads upstairs, and continue on down the bright, wide-open hallway, connecting to a separate wing of the house.

We enter a splendid, stately room. There's an older man and an older lady standing near the unlit fire place, and a stunning blonde sitting gracefully on the brocade sofa.

The older couple seems incredibly distressed. The blonde bombshell stands and elegantly struts toward Dominic.

I notice that Dominic's posture changes. His shoulders straighten and he lifts his chin in a decidedly challenging pose.

"What the fuck are you doing here?" he says angrily. He glares at the woman.

"Darling, it's your birthday. We always come to your parents' home for your birthday. Happy thirty-ninth." She leans in and kisses his cheek.

"Why did you let her in?" he ignores the woman and growls at his parents.

I assume this is Chelsea, Dominic's ex-wife.

"We're so sorry, son. She said you invited her and that you're on good terms now."

"Oh darling, I've missed you." She moves her piercing blue eyes over to me, and looks me up and down. Her lip curls up in a sneer. "You mean you left me for that?" She points to me in a condescending manner.

"I left you because you're a liar and a manipulator." Dominic's clipped tone barely conceals his rage.

She turns away slightly and waves her hand dismissively. "Oh please, it was just a small misunderstanding that you took to heart. And really, look at her. Is she retarded? She hasn't said a word, just stands there gaping at me."

"Enough!" Dominic yells.

He lets go of my hand and I feel the loss of his contact and warmth.

He wraps his hand around the top of her arm and forcefully tugs her toward the front door.

"You do not come here, into my parents' home, and create a scene. You do not have any right to look at my girlfriend and say anything about her. Ever. Do you understand?"

"You'll beg me to come back. She's ugly. I'm beautiful," Chelsea says with supreme confidence.

"She's extraordinary. Now fuck off and don't come back, because I'll have a restraining order slapped on you so fast you damn well won't know what hit you. You got my money, and it's quite obvious you're spending it if that's your car outside. There's nothing more for you here, Chelsea."

"But, Dom, I love you," she says with what sounds like a practiced and plastic pout.

I hear the front door slam shut seconds after her statement and I stand looking awkwardly at his parents.

She's right though. In comparison to her, I really am ugly.

From what Dominic's told me about her, though, she's not half the person that I am.

Internal ugliness can be masked by external beauty only until that ugly is exposed. And right now, she's brought to light just what a horrid person she truly is.

"I'm so sorry." Dominic whispers in my ear as he takes my hand and leads me away from his parents.

We step into what I assume is a study, and he closes the door.

"I didn't know she was going to be here. I'm really sorry, Allyn. What she said about you was completely uncalled for." He rubs his hands up and down my arms as he ducks his head down to look into my eyes.

"It's not your fault, so please forget it. I don't want to stay in here while your parents are waiting to wish you a happy birthday."

I turn to leave, but Dominic pulls me back into his arms.

"I love you, and only you. Kiss me," he softly commands. I can't help but lift my head to accept his warm lips on mine.

His hand cups my cheek as his thumb gently strokes the skin under my eye. His body curls against me.

"Come on," he says as he brings our foreheads together. "I'd really like my mom and dad to meet you." He kisses my cheek.

"Okay," I mumble as we walk out of the room holding hands.

The moment we're back in the family room, Dominic's mother gathers me in a strong embrace and whispers apologies.

"I'm so sorry, Allyn. That woman is vile. This is the first time I've ever seen her act like that. I can't tell you how sorry I am." She hugs me closer then steps back to look at me. "Please forgive us, we really didn't know."

"Please Mrs. Shriver, you aren't to blame."

"It's Doris, and this is John." She holds her hand out to her husband and Dominic's father.

John walks toward me and shakes my hand.

"It's a pleasure to meet you, Allyn," he says and looks quite uncomfortable.

I quickly check my hair and find that my right ear is exposed, which is apparently making him feel awkward. I rearrange my hair so they can't see my ear and turn to look at Dominic.

"Oscar's not here yet?" Dominic asks, filling a harsh silence.

"No he called and said he's running late and to go ahead and have dinner without him. He said he'll be here for cake though," Doris says. "Come on kids, let's go have dinner."

John indicates for Dominic and me to go ahead of him, and he quietly follows behind us.

The dining room is an extension of the serene and beautiful décor I've seen in the rest of the house.

Dominic pulls my chair out and I sit, and he takes his place next to me. John and Doris sit opposite us and still look unsettled at what's transpired this evening.

I feel a little on display, like I need to impress them, but I can tell that they're fairly quiet people too.

"Tell us, Allyn, what do you do?" Doris innocently asks.

"Um, I don't work anymore," I reply softly, hoping she doesn't ask me why.

Dominic's hand on my thigh tightens and I look over to find him smiling at me.

"Dominic says you live close to him," John says as their butler places a flat, white plate in front of me. There's a round, pinkish mound on it. "Yes, he lives only a few minutes from me."

I look over to Dominic and wait until he tells me what it is.

"It's tuna tartare, one of my favorites," he whispers.

I reach for my fork to taste it. It's quite subtle and delicious, so I happily eat it.

"Have you ever travelled, Allyn? Doris and I love to discover new places. There aren't a lot of states we haven't visited in America." He turns to his wife. "Do you remember the time we took the boys to the Grand Canyon and Dominic decided he wanted to bring that hurt lizard back with us?" Doris starts chuckling and I can't help but laugh along at the contagious sound.

"It's not true," Dominic says, interrupting the laughter.

"Oh it is, Allyn. Dominic found a lizard that had been clipped by something and it was trying to move. He picked the damn thing up and brought it over to his mother and said, 'Mommy I can fix him.' Doris jumped through the roof and Oscar started arguing with Dominic, telling him to put it down or he'd get rabies. I was laughing so hard," John says. Doris and I are laughing and Dominic has his own rueful smile as he continues to eat his entrée.

"It wasn't like that," Dominic says.

"It certainly was exactly like that. How old was Dominic then? About eight, Doris?"

"I was ten and Oscar was nine. And I could have saved the lizard."

That statement alone is enough to make us all laugh even harder.

"Dominic, I need to use the bathroom," I whisper, trying not to alert his parents.

"I'll show you," he says and stands to move my chair out for me.

"Excuse me," I say to his parents. They're both too busy laughing at their son to really notice us leaving the table.

"It's this way," Dominic points out as he holds my hand.

"Your parents are really funny."

"I think they were nervous about meeting you, but let me tell you, that the whole lizard thing? I definitely could've saved it."

I giggle again at him.

As we walk down the hallway, I hear the front door close and a deep voice call, "I'm here." Then, lower, "Hang on, I just got to my parents' house."

"Oh, Oscar's here. I can't wait for you to meet him. It sounds like he's on the phone with someone. I'll introduce you when you come out of the bathroom."

"Ha, yeah, you're hilarious," says Oscar in a deep gravelly voice, talking to the person on the phone. "Well, you best shut that cunt up then, eh?"

I notice that distinct tang in his voice, almost like a country singer. He rolls the N in his word, like his tongue stays connected with the roof of his mouth for a moment too long. I know that voice; I hear it in my nightmares.

I freeze, completely unable to move.

Cold washes over me.

My throat closes and my stomach spasms, wanting to expel everything inside it.

"Allyn, you're trembling."

I can't breathe.

My panic button, where's my panic button? Where the fuck is my panic button?!

I feel something wet run down my leg. I look down, horrified, at the puddle beneath me on the hardwood floor. I've wet myself.

My body begins to shut down.

Black spots cloud my eyes.

It's him.

He's found me.

He'll kill me.

I collapse.

TWENTY-SEVEN

Dominic

WHAT THE FUCK?

Allyn collapses. Luckily, I'm standing next to her and I instinctively reach out to catch her in my arms before she hits the floor.

"Allyn," I say loudly, trying to rouse her from her unconscious state.

What the hell just happened?

I replay the last few seconds in my head as I lift her and take her to the sofa. Her skirt is drenched and I look down to see she's lost control of her bladder.

I take a few steps and stop.

"Mom," I yell urgently. She comes running out to the foyer and looks around frantically. "Take care of Allyn."

I know what's happened. There's only one thing that could frighten her badly enough to wet herself and pass out.

Part of my education taught me to understand how a victim of abuse reacts when confronted by an abuser.

I place Allyn on the sofa and don't stop to worry about her wet clothes. There's a throw on the back of the sofa and I cover her with it.

Fuck. Now I know Oscar had a part in Allyn's attack.

Oscar's standing in the hallway, at the edge of the family room. He's still talking on the phone as I lunge for him. He doesn't see the punch coming before my fist makes contact with his goddamn chin.

"What the fuck did you do?" I shout at him.

"Nothing. What the fuck's wrong with you?" he says as he stumbles back. Understanding starts to dawn in his eyes. His phone is still in his hand. "Wait, let me make a call." I grab the phone and throw it against the wall. It smashes and pieces fly in all different directions.

I don't give him a chance to say another fucking word, I grab him by the collar and start smashing his face, not holding anything back.

He hits me with an uppercut, causing me to stumble back and lose my hold on him.

"I didn't do anything," he screams, holding his hands up in a defensive stance.

"It was you," I yell and charge at him again.

I pin him against the wall and keep punching him until I can feel the fight leaving his body.

"What are you talking about?" he chokes out between punches to the face and abdomen. His face is bloodied. His eye is quickly swelling, and my knuckles have split. They hurt like I've broken my hand.

I don't care about the pain. I push past it and pummel him repeatedly until I feel someone pulling me off of him.

I turn to attack the motherfucker tugging me away from Oscar and I see my father's face. He's shocked, but I see guilt and something like regret flash through his eyes before he lets me go and backs away with his palms up. He's terrified. But I don't think it's me he's afraid of.

I'm petrified that I wouldn't have stopped if he hadn't intervened.

I look over my shoulder at Oscar; he's slumped on the floor and twisting around, cradling his stomach. After a sharp moment of silence, sounds erupt in the room all at once. I can hear my mother sobbing and crying. My father keeps repeating, "Calm down, Dominic." And my brother is whimpering.

My blood is beyond boiling, and my heart's racing. Anger and fury pump through me, wanting me to tear Oscar apart.

"We called 911," my father says in a calmer tone.

Allyn.

I see her on the sofa, and my heart breaks. She looks so small and helpless lying still, and I go to her.

"Sweetheart," I say but my tone comes out quite hoarse and angry.

I need to calm myself down.

I kneel beside her and stroke her hair and kiss her forehead.

"Sweetheart," I repeat in a much calmer voice. "You can come back now, I won't let him hurt you again." She doesn't stir. "Open your eyes and look at me. I need you to tell me that you love me." I keep my eyes steady on her face. Not a damn flicker, not a twitch, nothing. She doesn't move. "I need you in my life, Allyn. You're my rare beauty, the precious gem that stole my heart and you can't ever give it back to me, because I won't take it. We brought color back into each other's lives the moment we met. I can't be without you." I stroke the soft skin on her face as I hover over her, and keep talking. "You have all of me, Allyn, and you have to come back to me." I kiss her cheek.

"Dominic, the ambulance and police should be here soon." Mom places a hand on my shoulder, and I nod my head, acknowledging her words. "What happened?" she asks, but I ignore her, focusing on Allyn.

"I only just found you, please don't go away. I couldn't breathe without you by my side. I need you with me." I gently lift my fingers to stroke her face softly and catch sight of my bloody hand.

I try and wipe the blood on my shirt. Allyn has had enough blood in her life without me adding to it.

"Dominic," my mother says as she moves next to me. I look at Mom, who's got tears trickling down her cheeks. "What happened, son?"

"He raped her three years ago. And she recognized his voice and collapsed."

"Your brother is a lawyer, Dominic. He took an oath to uphold the law. Why would he have done that to Allyn?" she asks.

I remember something that Lauren told me when I first asked to get me information on Allyn. There were so many girls and only two survived, one of whom took her life shortly after she was found.

"She's not the only one, Mom. There were a lot of others. Allyn is the only survivor though." I look down at Allyn and lift her hand against my face and run her palm along my cheek, comforted by the feel of her soft, pale skin.

"Wait, this was a few years back if I remember correctly." Mom's eyebrows furrow together and she bites her lip in frustration as she looks like she's trying to remember something.

"Three years." I look around the room and don't see Dad. "Where's Dad?" I ask Mom.

"He's looking after your brother."

Every hair follicle stands on end when Mom relates me to Oscar. "He's no brother of mine."

"Dominic, this might all be a misunderstanding. It might not have been him. You can't come to such a drastic conclusion without even giving him the benefit of explaining."

"I don't have to give him anything. Allyn's body told me all I need to know. Mom, she heard his voice and lost control of her bladder."

"Is she wet?" Mom asks and pulls the covers back.

"Yeah she is."

"I've got some new panties, still in the plastic, and some sleep pants that will fit her. I'll go get them." Mom rushes out of the room.

I turn back to Allyn.

"Come on, sweetheart. We have a lifetime of memories to make, and we can't do that if you won't open your eyes." I drop my voice and whisper in her ear, "I'll always protect you. You'll never feel pain again as long as I'm close to you."

"Dominic," Mom says, taking my attention away from my girl.

"I love you more than my own life," I whisper as I kiss her on the cheek and run my hand up and down her arm.

"I'll get her cleaned up and changed, son. Go and see to your hand."

"No, Mom, I'll take care of her."

Mom bites on her lip and turns to leave.

I undress Allyn, wiping her with the dry part of the skirt I just took off her. I take the panties out of the packaging and slip them on her, then get her legs into the sleep pants and pull them up over her hips. I pick her up and move her to the other sofa, wrapping her up in the blanket. I don't want her waking and becoming embarrassed when the police and paramedics arrive. She needs to retain as much dignity as she can during this very difficult time for her.

"Mom," I call.

"Do you need help, Dominic?"

"No it's done. But I need you to take her clothes and put them in a bag in case the police need them. I don't think she'll ever want to see them again. If the police don't need them, throw them away, or destroy them, I don't care."

"Alright, I'll wait for them to tell me what to do with them. Look, if your brother…"

"He's not my brother. He did this."

"If he did, then he'll be dealt with by the law."

I run my bloodied hands through my hair then over my face. "Not if I get to him first."

"Dominic," my father calls from his position next to Oscar.

I get up and walk out to find my father opening the door to four policemen.

They flash a glance at Oscar laying bloodied on the floor, then to me. They see my cracked, blood-covered hands. Immediately one draws his gun and yells at me to lie face down on the floor with my arms outstretched and palms facing down.

I comply with their demands and one approaches and cuffs me.

"I'm gonna help you up," he says as he tugs on my arms as I lift myself. Another police officer stands in front of me.

"I'm Officer Sweeney. What happened to him?" he asks me.

"I beat the shit out of him," I answer.

"Looks that way. Now why did you do that?"

"Because he raped my girlfriend." Sweeney's eyebrows rise in surprise.

The paramedics arrive and see Oscar on the floor, moaning in pain.

Fucker, I should've killed him.

He turns and gives Sweeney a small nod.

"Don't worry about him, get my girlfriend to the hospital. She's over there." I jut my chin toward the family room. "She passed out and I can't wake her up."

One of the paramedics goes to her and I'm relieved to know she's being cared for.

"Make sure he's cuffed," Sweeney instructs one of the other police officers as he's looking at Oscar.

"Mom, go with Allyn. If she wakes up before I'm released, tell her I'll be there the moment I can."

"Of course," she says as she kisses my cheek.

"Let's take this back to the station and get it sorted," Sweeney says and leads me out the door.

Sandwiched between two police officers, I'm pushed and pulled out the front door.

Getting further and further away from my beautiful, courageous Allyn.

TWENTY-EIGHT

Dominic

"**M**R. SHRIVER, YOUR FATHER IS HERE TO SEE YOU," A YOUNG female police officer announces as Dad walks in behind her.

I've been sitting in this cold, sterile room for the better part of an hour. The handcuffs are off, but I still feel caged in here.

No one's taken my statement yet. I have no idea what's happening beyond this room. No one has told me anything about Allyn's condition, or Oscar's. Not that I care about him.

"Dad," I say as I stand and walk toward him. "What's happened to Allyn?"

"Thank you." My father graciously thanks the police officer and she steps out, closing the door behind her.

"Dad?"

"Son, we've got a few things to talk about." Dad sits down in the chair opposite to the one I was sitting in. He leans his elbows on the table and hangs his head, as if he's dreading this conversation.

I catch another glimpse of some unknown emotion in his eyes, something I've never seen him express before. Suddenly, I know what he's feeling.

Shame.

"What's going on?" I sit down and lean across to Dad to touch his hand.

"Don't," he says, pulling his hand away. His voice loaded with so much remorse and sorrow.

"Is Allyn alright? Has something happened to her? I swear, if something's happened I will end him," I spit through a tightly clenched jaw as I get up and start pacing, unable to remain still. "I will fucking kill him if...if... fuck!" I turn and punch the wall out of anger and frustration. That sick fuck.

"Calm down, Dominic. It's nothing like that. I talked to your mother before I came in here. We got her a private room at the hospital, and Allyn's comfortable, but she's not awake yet. Your mother and I are taking care of all her medical costs."

My fist already hurts from laying into Oscar, but now, thanks to my outburst, the pain has intensified. I think I may have broken a knuckle. But I don't care about that; I just have a raw and uncontrollable need to hurt the man who's hurt Allyn.

Then I reconsider my father's words. "Hang on. Why did you set her up in a private room?" I ask, curious. They only met Allyn tonight. They aren't any more responsible for Oscar's actions then I am. Why are they suddenly so concerned about her?

Unless...

Dad's ashamed.

My parents have accepted her medical expenses.

My father has something to tell me.

Their reaction when I beat Oscar, and told them what he did to Allyn was, for the lack of a better word, calm. Accepting.

I flop back down in the chair, and pray to every God ever known to man that I'm simply over-thinking this and that they didn't know about Oscar. About what he did to the woman I brought to their home.

Because if they did, they're just as responsible as he is. Worse. They should be arrested too. Why, if they knew, did they do nothing about it?

"Dad?" I ask in a quiet voice, not wanting to ask, but needing to know.

Dad looks across at me and quickly looks away, unable to hold my gaze. That fleeting look of guilt I saw earlier is plastered on his face. It can no longer be hidden.

His shoulders slump and his brows knit together as he takes a deep breath.

"Please tell me you and Mom didn't know about this," I plead with him. Please let me be imagining this shit.

Dad says nothing.

Not a goddamn fucking word.

He's hiding his face but his body language is radiating shame and guilt.

"Dad, I need to know," I say more forcefully but silently hoping it's not true.

He nods his head once, the smallest of nods. No, that's not good enough. I need to hear the words.

"Dad, tell me the truth," I say still praying that I've got it wrong.

"When your brother…"

"He's not my brother," I cut him off.

He sighs. "When Oscar was in his last year of high school and you were in the first year of college, Oscar came home saying that a girl at school was accusing him of rape. He said that she was going to go to the police and tell them about it unless he turned himself in."

What? Why didn't she go to the police? Why was she warning him of what she was going to do? That makes no sense at all.

"So we got in contact with the girl and paid her off. Quite handsomely, too."

"So she just wanted money?" I shake my head in disbelief that anyone could be so callous, to trade all that pain just for money.

"It appeared so at the time."

My eyes fly to Dad. He's still not looking at me. He's staring at a spot on the table that only he can see.

"What does that mean?" My knee is bouncing and I'm chewing on the inside of my cheek, restraining my every unbearable urge to get up and pound into Dad.

"Oscar denied even being sexually active with her, until she wound up pregnant. That's when she came back for money."

"I don't believe a sixteen- or seventeen-year-old girl would have the intelligence to scheme something like that," I say. Truly, this shit is unbelievable.

"Her parents found out about the baby. When she told them what happened, the father came to the house ready to turn Oscar in. I bought their silence."

"Just like that?" I ask shaking my head.

"Yes, just like that."

"But that could've been just a stupid decision not use a condom while they were having sex. That didn't prove that Oscar raped her," I say trying against my own better judgment to find justification for something that had none. Something convinced my parents that the girl's accusations were true, and I need to know what that was.

"You're right, it doesn't. But when I sat down with Oscar and talked to him about it, he admitted he'd lied to me and that they did have sex. And that the sex was very rough and that the girl liked to be smacked around."

My mind is going around and around in confusion. None of this makes any sense.

"How did I not know about this?" My hands go up in exasperation.

"Because you were away at college, and we protected you. We didn't want you involved in something so…" he stops talking to think of an appropriate word. "Inconsequential."

"A girl claiming she's raped is not something that should be bought off or swept under the rug. Your son was accused of something not only illegal, but also disgusting and immoral. And you totally disregarded it?"

Dad looks around the room, still not meeting my angry glare.

Shit.

There's more.

I can tell by his body language that it's more than just this one event.

"What else?" I ask coldly.

"It sort of happened again in college."

"Sort of? What does sort of mean?"

"Well, in his third year of college, I got a call from a police officer who wanted to meet with me in a public place to talk about Oscar. When we met that day, he told me that he had taken a report from a girl who wanted to press charges against Oscar for raping her.

"She said that they were at a party and Oscar slipped her a date rape drug, that he took her back to his apartment, raped her, and allowed a friend to rape her. She said she was in and out of consciousness but remembers Oscar and some other guy she couldn't describe. When she woke up, she was lying in an alley, partially clothed. She went home and showered and a few days later a friend showed her some photos she'd taken on her phone. There was one of her and Oscar, and it jogged her memory enough that she remembered part of what happened.

"She went to the police and the case was being handled by this police officer, Michael I think his name was. Anyway, the cop recognized Oscar's surname, knew he came from money, and basically, for seven figures, the case disappeared."

What the fuck did I just hear?

Is this a fucking joke?

"What happened to the girl?"

"I never asked, Dominic. I just said that I never wanted to hear about it again."

Who are these people that call themselves my family?

"Did you ask Oscar about it?" I ask in total disbelief. Really, I'm astonished.

"I did." He nods his head but goes on to say, "And he said she liked it rough, too."

My mouth falls open, as Dad swipes at a tear.

"Why did you protect him?"

"I protected all of us."

"No fucking way. I don't need protection; I've never done anything wrong. Does Mom know?"

Please say no.

"Of course. Your mother was the one who told me both times to pay them whatever they were asking."

Well this shit's just gotten unbelievable.

"How can you sit there and shed a fucking tear when you knew all along what he was capable of? You knew what he did to those girls, and you paid them off for silence." I stand up and ball my already aching hand into fists. I'm so fucking pissed off, so tense that I can feel the muscles in my arms vibrating with sheer, fucking fury.

"We did it to protect you."

"Bullshit! You did it to protect yourselves. You think that because the name Shriver is attached to bonds and stocks all over the world that it gives your son the right to do what he wants with girls? How many has he killed because you were trying to 'protect' us?"

"Son," he starts saying.

"Don't call me that. I'm no longer related to you. This so-called family is completely devoid of any sense of decency and I don't want to be associated with any of you. How do you aim on fixing this one? Because guess what, John? I fully intend to get up in that witness stand and tell the judge and the jury everything you just said, along with everything I know about that weak, pathetic excuse for a son you have. And don't think I'm doing this for Allyn. I'm doing this for every victim that he raped and broke for his own demonic enjoyment before he killed them. And I'm doing this because it's the right thing to do – something you're apparently incapable of."

"Dominic, you have to think about what you just said. This will affect you too. Your name will be tarnished and you'll be investigated." He's beginning to panic now, because he knows I meant every word.

Are you fucking kidding me?

The only word I can really use at this instant is, stunned.

Stunned at his audacity in asking me to remain quiet.

Stunned at how he would rather his rapist son go free to harm more innocent women.

Stunned at how little remorse he's showing.

But mostly, stunned that he thinks I'm that sort of man.

I may have my flaws, but I won't hide behind money in fear of retribution.

"They can investigate anything they like. I have nothing to hide and nothing to be ashamed of."

"Really? You're screwing one of your head case patients."

I can't help it. I really can't. I just do it.

I leap over the table and land a couple of punches to his face.

"You don't talk about her," I yell as someone pulls me off that useless, lying piece of garbage that I was once proud to call my father.

"Get the father out of here," Sweeney yells at one of the other officers.

I sit back down and try to stretch my right hand out but wince in pain. Nope, something's definitely broken.

"What the hell happened?" Sweeney asks.

"I found out my so-called family is based on lies," I grind out between clenched teeth.

"Does this have anything to do with your brother?" He sits down.

"Yeah, it does, and you'll need to record my statement for evidence."

A paramedic comes in to look at my hand, wraps it, and says I'll need to go to the hospital soon to have it x-rayed. I choose to fight though the pain and give my statement first. Sweeney leaves the room and a tall, nondescript man enters.

He introduces himself as Detective Harrison. Harrison turns to look at the one way glass and gives a small nod that must be their signal to start recording.

The initial identification questions give me time to calm down and think about what I need to tell them.

"Tell me about Oscar," Detective Harrison starts.

"I just learned that this all began when he was seventeen years old."

And now the world will know, too.

TWENTY-NINE

I CAN HEAR A BEEP, AND PEOPLE TALKING CLOSE TO ME. MY EYES flutter open and immediately close, in protest against the brightness and glare.

"Sweetheart." I know immediately it's Dominic. His hand is covering mine and he gently squeezes it. I feel his warm, slightly moist lips carefully touch the back of my hand with a sweet kiss. "Can you hear me?" he asks and kisses my hand again.

"Hmmm," is the only sound I can muster. My throat's dry and it feels like it's been rubbed with gravel. It's painful to swallow.

"I'm here, my beautiful Allyn. I'm here."

My eyes flutter open again and slowly adjust to the brilliance of the room. The room is small and sterile, with plain white walls and a big window that overlooks the parking lot. The pane is tinted but the sun outside is quite bright, and looks happy today, touching everyone with its magnificent rays.

I look over and see Dominic's brown eyes examining me with concern and love.

"How are you feeling?" he asks in a soft, serene tone brushing my hair away from my face.

I swallow again until my mouth has a little moisture and start to say,

"I'm alright." My voice is weak and cracks, but at least I'm talking. "What happened?" I ask hoarsely.

"We were at my parents' house, remember?" Dominic starts, pouring me a cup of water and handing it to me.

That's all he's said and every second rushes back.

My body stiffens and shakes as I recall hearing him on the phone.

I'm panting so quickly that the rate of my heart beat seems unhealthy, even to me. A panic attack hovers, waiting to swoop down on me. Dominic takes the water cup from me to prevent it spilling. He raises it to my dry lips and I drink greedily.

"One, two, three, four, breathe in through your nose."

I look over to Dominic and let his deep baritone begin to calm me.

I take a breath in through my nose and close my eyes.

"Five, six, seven, eight, nine and breathe out through your mouth."

I open my eyes and reach out with my free hand to hold onto Dominic, and I don't let go. He's been my absolute anchor from the moment I met him. He's been incredibly supportive and has never let me fail.

Now is no different.

"What day is today?" I say as I try and figure out how long I've been here.

"It's Tuesday. You've been out since Sunday. The doctors said that you went into shock, and your brain shut down to protect you."

I let go of him and rub my hands over my face.

"What happened with your brother?" I ask. But suddenly I notice a bandage on Dominic's hand as I look over at him. "What happened to your hand?" I cry, fearful that he was hurt because of me.

"I beat Oscar, that's what happened to my hand. And he's no longer my brother. As a matter of fact, I've disowned all of them. I'll never go back there again. They're no longer my family. You are." Dominic stands and starts pacing the length of the room, back and forth. With every step, he gets angrier.

"What happened?" I ask carefully, not wanting to trigger any further anger. I know he won't hurt me; he'd never hurt me. But I can tell that this conversation is not going to be easy for him. He stops pacing and takes a deep breath.

"Alright. First of all, Oscar's been arrested for your attack and rape."

I take a huge breath and my heart hammers against my chest.

"It was the bite mark on your shoulder that put him at the scene."

I look toward where the bite mark is on my shoulder, but of course, it's covered by the hospital gown and I can't see it. "I don't understand. How?"

Dominic comes to me. He lifts his hip to sit on the edge of the small hospital bed and takes my hand. "When you were first found, 911 was called. The police took impressions of the bite marks, along with other evidence. The case went cold, but the evidence was kept."

"Alright," I acknowledge Dominic's words.

"Then when you passed out Sunday night, I knew from your reaction that Oscar was involved. Doris took care of you, while I beat Oscar until he was nothing more than the scum he is."

He called his mom Doris, not mom. I wait patiently as he continues his recollection of events. "Doris and John asked me what happened and I told them."

"Okay, but I don't understand why you're not on speaking terms with them any longer."

"Allyn," he whispers and shakes his head. "This is seriously fucked up. It's actually beyond being fucked up, it's just completely wrong on so many levels."

He looks so stressed and it's causing me to worry, because I really don't know what the hell is going on.

"Just tell me," I say as I reach for his face and lightly run my palm down his cheek.

"Your touch makes everything better." He leans into me and kisses my forehead with a precious small kiss.

A small rumble comes from him and I crave his warmth, the power of how I feel when he's holding me. I just want to be held in his safe, protective arms, and never leave them.

He closes his eyes and takes a deep breath. When he opens them he looks so, sad.

"I love you," I say as I stare up into his eyes. "But, please tell me what happened."

"They knew all along what sort of person he is, and they paid off two of his past victims in exchange for their silence. They used their money to keep him out of jail. They both knew, and he told them that his victims liked to be slapped around and enjoyed rough sex. After the second time, John and Doris told him they'd disown him if it happened again. That's when he started killing his victims so they couldn't come back to accuse him."

I wince at his words, and remember the brutal, vicious, sadistic way they hurt me. They gave no thought to me at all, like I was nothing more than a waste of air.

Laughing at me.

Urinating on me.

Forcing their disgusting cocks into me.

Forcing a knife inside me while they had me spread open and tied down.

I shiver, remembering what they did to me. "Why would they protect him?" Bile is rising in my throat and I exercise all my control not to gag.

"Two reasons, and neither of them are justifiable in my eyes. Their name and their money. They didn't want their name splashed across every major newspaper in America, and they didn't want to lose their money. They thought if they could buy his victims off, they wouldn't have to face the consequences. They tried with you, but I wouldn't allow them to keep protecting him, to let him free to ruin anymore lives."

"But there was at least another one with Oscar. There was a Mick." I remember it like it was yesterday.

"When I laid into Oscar, he was talking to someone on the phone, but I took it and smashed it. I told the police everything, Allyn, including that he was in the middle of a phone call, and they're doing what they have to, to find this Mick."

"And what's happened to Oscar?"

"He confessed earlier today. He's working with police to identify the others that he and his friends took."

I feel my forehead crinkle and I'm overwhelmed by the questions crowding my brain. Right now, though, I need to keep my head in the right space, and hopefully everything will be revealed in time.

"He's talking to the police about the other girls that were taken, but he hasn't told them who was with him? Why?"

Dominic shrugs his shoulders. "I don't know. I haven't spoken to Oscar, and I'm not going to. I've washed my hands of all of them."

I lean into Dominic and wrap him in a hug as he holds me close.

It feels like only a moment passes before there's a knock on the door and it creaks open.

A tall man comes in, closes the door behind him, and moves to the opposite corner of the room, essentially as far away from me as possible.

I hide behind Dominic and look at the man sideways, not knowing who he is or why he's here.

"Detective Harrison, how are you today?" Dominic says to the man with cropped, light brown hair. He's a little pudgy around the middle, but he carries it well and it doesn't diminish his intimidating stance.

"Good, Dominic, thanks." The detective looks at me and I move so I'm hidden from him.

"Allyn, this is the detective that took my statement. He won't hurt you, and I won't leave your side." He strokes my hair with the palm of his hand and pushes the strands behind my ear and down my back.

"Hi Allyn, I'm Simon. Is it okay if I take a couple of steps toward you?" he asks as he holds his hands up in surrender to show me he's not a threat to me.

I peek around Dominic's shoulder and nod to him. I watch as he takes one small step and waits for me to approve another.

I nod my head and he shuffles two steps closer to me, then stops a few feet away from the bottom of the bed. I shake my head and he doesn't move any closer.

"You're doing so well. I can't tell you how much I love your strength," Dominic whispers and pecks me on the lips.

"Allyn, I'm sure Dominic has filled you in with what's been happening?"

"Yeah, he was just telling me."

"Oscar will be going to jail, most likely for the rest of his natural life."

"He deserves hell, not jail," I say with the scorn in my tone.

"You're right, he does. But I'm here to ask you some questions to make sure we can put him away." He looks at me warily, like I'm fragile and about to shatter.

I look at him and wait for his question.

175

"Do you know a Michael Greene?" he asks.

I look away from him. Michael is the name of Faith's boyfriend, but I can't remember if she told me his last name.

"The only Michael I know of is my friend Faith's boyfriend, but I don't know his surname," I tell Simon.

"What's your friend's last name?" He takes a little black notebook out of his back pocket and flicks through the pages.

Dominic's fingers tighten around my hand and I look at him noticing how tense and angry his face is. He's scowling and he looks like he wants to say something, but is waiting for me to answer Simon's question.

"Um, Faith's last name is Collins."

Simon looks at his pad, and then looks at me.

"Where can I find Miss Collins? Do you know her address?" He takes a pen from his shirt pocket.

"When I spoke to her she said her boyfriend had asked her to move in with him, but she wasn't sure about it. So she'd probably still be with her parents. Lemongrove Road on the other side of town. But I don't understand. What do you want with her Michael? Do you need his help with the investigation? She told me he's a police officer."

"Not exactly, Allyn. We need to question him, but when we went to his apartment he wasn't there and called in sick today."

Dominic looks at me, then over at Simon, then back at me. "Is he the crooked cop that asked John for money?" he asks Simon as he moves his body to support me.

"I believe he is, but Oscar just indicated that he's one of the other men that raped you, Allyn. There's one more too. A low-life drug addict named Rocky Adams. He was the one who chose the victims."

I feel my mouth fall open and suddenly the thunder crashes down within me. I'm sent into oblivion, and I can't parse all this fucked-up information pelting me. I sink into bed and cover my entire body with the blanket, and turn toward the wall, just shutting everything out and not wanting to listen anymore.

Faith wanted to bring that beast into my home and introduce us, and it turns out he was one of them. There were three, a police officer, an attorney and a junkie.

"How many?" I ask from beneath the blankets. I don't want to ask but

I have to know. "How many girls?" I question just a little louder.

"You don't need to know," Dominic says as he strokes long gentle movements up and down my back.

I flip the covers down and turn back to look at the two men. Suddenly I burst into angry tears and can't help but feel sorry for myself and all the others. "How many?!" I shout.

"Thirty-six girls that we know of," Simon says then quickly averts his eyes and looks down at his notebook.

Thirty-six.

What a horrific and utterly devastating number.

My mind goes completely numb. My eyes droop closed, and I turn off the world.

THIRTY

"**A**LLYN, THEY'RE DISCHARGING YOU. WE CAN GO HOME."
I turn over in the bed and look up at Dominic. His handsome features smile down at me and he tilts his head to the side to look into my eyes.

"Will you stay with me?" I plead with him.

"I'm not going anywhere if you aren't beside me, in this life or any other."

I smile at Dominic and sit up in bed.

"I feel so tired, Dominic. My body, my mind, and my soul. They all just need to rest."

"Come on. I'll take you home and we can stay in bed for as long as you want." Dominic reaches his hand out to me in a welcoming gesture, and I look at it and consider pulling the blankets back over my head and shutting the world out again. "We can heal together at home where we're both comfortable, not in this tiny bed where I can't even hold you in my arms."

I lower my gaze to the floor and I take a deep breath.

He's right, of course. This hospital isn't a place for me to heal. I've been here for six days and all I get is nurses coming in and bothering me with stupid questions and feigned concern. I understand they've got a job to do, but I also know that I'm not going to get better care here than what I would at home with Dominic by my side.

"Okay, let's go home," I reply to his heartfelt words. "Let me change first." I throw the covers back and go to the overnight bag Dominic brought me. I didn't have an overnight bag before, but Dominic went and bought one, filling it with new clothes, a toothbrush, and everything else he thought I might need.

"I'll be right outside. Take your time." He leans down and kisses my forehead before turning and leaving the small, stark hospital room.

I quickly get changed and when I open the door, Dominic's standing guard on the other side.

"You ready?" he asks as he comes back into the room.

"I've just got to get my toothbrush and toiletries."

"Leave them, I've already stocked up on everything at home. Come on, let's go."

He takes my overnight bag and loops his arm around my waist, pulling me close to him as he opens the door.

"Wait, I have to make arrangements for the hospital bill," I say as I turn toward reception.

"It's been taken care of." Dominic pulls me in the direction of the parking lot.

"No, they haven't come in to see me yet. I need to give them my insurance details and organize a payment plan."

"I paid for it," he says confidently.

What?

"You don't have to do that." I look up at him as he guides me through the maze of hospital corridors.

"No, I don't have to. I choose to. Because I love you and I want you with me forever. I fully intend on supporting you, whether that be financially, emotionally or physically."

"Thank you," I whisper, surrendering to his generous and protective nature.

When we get to the car, Dominic, as usual, opens the door for me.

We drive home in silence, and I watch as dark, angry clouds seem to follow us. It's not raining, but the threat seems imminent. I know, deep down inside, that the dark clouds are waiting to strike, determined to keep me in my old, fear-based mindset. Never letting me move on or truly recover. So much has changed, but this remains the same.

They hang low in the sky, watching my every movement with an observant, evil eye. The loathsome gray is heartless and cruel as it tries to remind me how broken I actually am.

I look around and think about these last few months.

Am I as insignificant as those clouds attempt to make me feel?

Has this situation made me retreat into myself and shut the world out again?

Yes, but only temporarily.

I'm much stronger than those puff balls want me to think I am. I've been to hell, not once, but twice and I'm still here.

Breathing and finally living.

Will my life ever be normal?

Define normal.

Will I ever be integrated fully back into society?

Highly unlikely.

Can I ever forget about that day that altered my universe?

Never, but I'm learning to manage it.

Is bearing a child so important to a relationship?

Maybe, but we'll have to find a way to deal with it.

I turn to Dominic and reach for his hand. A welcome current passes between our hands and I notice a tingle traveling down my back, all the way to my toes.

"Are you alright?" he asks without turning his head.

"You know what? I think I will be." I gently squeeze his hand and smile as he tightens his long fingers around mine.

When we get home, Dominic pulls up in front of the house and before I have a chance to open the door, he's standing by the car, smiling proudly with his hand outstretched.

We walk hand in hand up to the porch and as Dominic unlocks the doors and turns the alarm off, I take the few steps back down to the lawn.

I slip off my shoes and let my feet feel the soft, plush green grass as I look up to the sky.

The angry clouds seem to have followed us. They congregate over our home, and they seem on the verge of screaming at me to remind me of my place in the world.

In the distance I see sharp, piercing electric bolts flying down toward the ground. I smile, because that's their warning to me. To make me cower, hide away, and never forget they are my rulers.

"I'm not afraid of you anymore," I whisper as my eyes narrow and warn them. "You can scream all you want. You can try and keep me down. But I'm not listening to you ever again. I'm taking my power back."

The deep rumble of the thunder answers me.

I straighten my back and smile even wider. "Show me your worst, because I've already seen the Devil and survived him. You're nowhere near as frightening."

A stab of lightning closes in over my home.

"Are you angry because I've finally figured it out? You can't make me hate myself any longer."

A boom from the clouds shrieks loudly in my ears.

I stand taller and prouder before the fury of the clouds.

"I take back my sanity, and I choose to live. Your anger is no longer my problem."

I take a deep breath as the sky crackles and yells, trying to bring me back into darkness.

"I win my life back. Goodbye," I laugh as I turn and walk to my front door.

Dominic's leaning up against the house with his hands in his pockets. Pride is radiating off his entire body. "Is it over?" he asks.

For a spilt second I consider his words carefully, "I think it is. I'm hoping they listen and stay away."

He grabs the bottom of my t-shirt and pulls me against his body; his hands roam over my back as I lean into him.

The twinge of lust that's always been beneath the surface, has increased into a constant flutter of incredible warmth. I'm craving him, and want him close to me.

Maybe we can try again to be intimate so we can fully belong to each other.

"Come, I'm thinking about taking you to dinner at our little Italian restaurant," Dominic says as we step inside.

I stop and turn to look at the clouds that no longer intimidate me. I smile at them. "I think I'd love to see what she has to offer tonight," I answer Dominic. I will hide away no longer.

I step inside and I'm completely stunned by what I see.

I can't believe it.

I have a huge smile on my face and I take in every single scrap of color that I can.

I have beautiful new contemporary furniture.

There are stains on woods, colors that sing, trimmings that are bright and inviting, and a large ornate mirror in the foyer.

The beige is gone.

And my family room is purple.

THIRTY-ONE

"**D**OMINIC," I SAY, TRYING TO BREAK HIS CONCENTRATION ON whatever sport he's watching.

"Yeah," he answers as he turns his head to me although his eyes don't leave the TV.

"Have you moved in with me? You don't seem to go to your house to sleep anymore, and you're always here. Not that I mind, but I think I'd like for it to be official. You know the whole, 'Allyn I'd like to move in with you,' thing."

He carefully lifts the remote and turns the TV off. He doesn't just mute the volume; he turns it off completely.

"So you want me to ask you if I can move in?" A small smile tugs at the corners of his lips as he tries to stay straight-faced.

Cheeky man, he's teasing me now.

"Well, the polite thing to do is wait to be asked." I can play along with him. I sit back on the sofa and look around my bright purple room, admiring it like I have been for the last five days. I can see out of the corner of my eye that Dominic shifts his weight and leans toward me, waiting for me to ask.

"Are you going to ask?" he says with a touch of worry in his voice.

"Ask what?" I reply, acting like I have no idea what he wants.

"Really?" He tilts his head to the side and his eyebrows fly up with a look of surprise. But it's all in fun.

"I have no idea what you're asking."

"Then I suppose it's best if I tell you what's going to happen."

"Tell me?" Huh, now he's telling me. "Pray tell your little secret then, oh mighty alpha."

His face beams with a smile and I can tell he liked that nickname. "Alpha...hmmm, I think you can call me that more often, Allyn." He chuckles, and I laugh too. "But in all seriousness, I belong anywhere you are. Wherever you choose to go, I won't follow you; I'll lead you by the best path."

"Wow," I whisper and lower my gaze to the floor. He's undone me.

"Yes, Allyn, I've moved in," he chuckles softly. "And now it can be official, because I love you, and want to be with you." He moves closer to me and reaches out to take my hand. "Don't look down. I want to see your hypnotic gray eyes, because they are in all of my most amazing memories."

Warmth spreads through my body, and I look up. A delicious thrill pulsates deep inside my belly and a spray of goose bumps spreads from the back of my neck all the way down my legs.

"I love you," I sigh as I move in to kiss Dominic.

Our mouths connect but this time's different.

Or maybe, I'm different.

It's time to bury those monsters deep in the ground and cover them in concrete, securing them where they belong, by Satan's side in hell.

I break the kiss and pull back from Dominic.

"Sorry, I got carried away," he apologizes as he sits back to give me room.

But distance isn't what I'm craving.

I take a deep breath, and gather every ounce of courage that I have. I stand from the sofa and extend my hand to Dominic.

"Where are we going?" His eyebrows are knit together in worry and his lips are in a tight, thin line.

"I'm taking you to bed." I inject some confidence into those words, although truly, I'm petrified. But the one thing I know for sure is that Dominic will never hurt me.

"You don't have to, Allyn. I can wait." He answers my unspoken fears.

"I'm ready to try."

He takes my hand and stands. His solid body towers over me, and I know how fortunate I am to have him in my life.

"Only if you're sure." He dips down and presses his mouth over mine.

He softly sweeps my lower lip with his tongue and gently strokes my jaw. It eases my nerves to accept his kiss.

"I'm sure," I whisper against his lips. "I want you, Dominic."

He releases me and silently turns around to lead me upstairs to our bedroom.

"This is going to be very slow. We're going to take our time. There's no wrong in our room, just you and me connecting our minds and bodies."

"I know, and I really want to try. I'm ready."

Dominic swoops down and kisses me as he captures my mouth with his.

"I love you, Dominic." It takes every ounce of self-confidence that I have to push him to our bed.

"Allyn," he mumbles as he stops kissing me. "I can wait if you have even the slightest doubt." He cradles my head in his hand as he kisses the tip of my nose.

"There's no doubt." I nervously look up into his lust-filled eyes.

"You have to tell me to stop if it gets to be too much."

"I will."

"I can wear a condom, whatever it is you need."

"We've already talked about this, Dominic. Please don't overthink it, or I may lose my courage."

He steps back a little but his eyes never leave mine. "Allyn, if you're not ready then I don't want to do this."

I close the distance he was trying to put between us and lay both my hands on his chest. "Please let me feel, let me feel the brilliant colors with you."

With a smile Dominic takes my hand and leads me to the center of our now serene, light green room.

"Don't look anywhere but my eyes. Okay?" he says as he kneels before me.

"Alright," I whisper, trembling with my own arousal and lustful need.

With flaming eyes and tender lips, Dominic leans forward and presses a kiss through my clothes onto my belly, just a little higher than my belly button. His hands grip my bottom and he pulls me to him.

He slowly moves his hands to the front of my jeans and with one small flick, he pops the top button. He leans down and brushes his luscious, warm mouth against my exposed skin.

I weave my fingers through his hair and gently tug as I play with his thick, dark strands.

"Hmmm," he groans as he kisses me in the same spot again, sucking a little of my skin into his mouth.

He pops the second button and moves his mouth a little further down, touching the top of my pelvic bone.

I pull on his hair a little harder and close my eyes as the wave of desire rips through me. A shiver of need pulses through me as my stomach flips with anticipation.

"Keep your eyes open, Allyn. I need to watch you." Dominic's voice is heavy with lust.

My eyes fly open and I look down to see Dominic watching me as he pops the third button and kisses me over my panties, inhaling deeply.

He slides my jeans down past my hips to my feet and I step out of them, all while his hands don't once leave my needy body.

When he stands, my eyes focus on his chest, rapidly rising and falling as his hands go to my waist to lift my t-shirt and find the bare skin beneath. I slide my hands under his shirt and move them up his back, slowly lifting the material.

Dominic lifts his arms and I reach up on my tip-toes to pull his shirt over his head.

I carelessly throw the shirt to the floor, and look at the sprinkling of dark hair on his chest. I step into his space and press a kiss over his heart.

My tongue traces the line around his nipple as Dominic moves his hand to my nape and closes his fingers in a fist in my hair. He's not forcing me, but guiding me to keep my wet tongue against his burning skin.

Warm becomes hot and sweet becomes intoxicating.

A rumble echoes from deep within his chest as I lovingly move to his other nipple, just sucking with the slightest pressure, moving my tongue with a teasing touch. He tightens his grip in my hair and keeps me where he wants me a little longer. Dominic lifts my head with his finger under my chin and drowns me in a kiss. His tongue massages mine, and his hands lift the edges of my t-shirt.

The intense connection of our kiss is momentarily broken as he takes my shirt off and drops it to the floor with his, creating a pile of abandoned clothes.

I'm standing in my panties and bra and look down to see all my disgusting scars highlighted against my pale skin that's flushing with excitement.

"Keep your eyes on mine," he rasps.

I nod once and look up at him.

With nervous fingers, I touch his chest and draw my hand down his stomach to the button on his jeans.

My touch is not as steady as his, but I manage to undo the button and zipper to slide his pants down his legs.

I want him.

I need him.

I need this.

The urgency to feel closer to Dominic is building and I'm yearning for more from him.

"I need to feel you," I say, my voice a breathy rasp.

His eyes are heavy-lidded with desire, a molten cloud over his dark, impassioned gaze.

Dominic moves to unclasp my bra and suddenly, I don't want him seeing me the way I am. I cover my breasts once my bra's taken off and step back, looking away from Dominic.

"You didn't hide from me at the pond, and I don't want you to hide from me now. What we're sharing is beautiful, just like the woman before me."

I'm shaking and my breathing has become quick, shaky, but for the wrong reason. He's going to hate what he sees. One of my breasts was almost hacked off and it's heavily scarred. My body is covered with carvings and marks.

"Please," he whispers. "Let me see all of you."

I stand rooted to the spot with tears welling, and my ears are filled with a heavy drumming sound echoing from deep within.

I drop my hands and let Dominic see my scars and my ugliness, up close for the first time.

"Perfect," he tenderly murmurs, just loud enough for me to hear.

With calm, determined movements, Dominic lifts his hands to touch my breasts. With his palms on each, he closes his hand around them and gently kneads them between his tepid fingers.

"Simply perfect," he repeats in a low voice.

A single damn tear falls down my cheek.

He really does love me. Otherwise, he would have left the moment he saw me without the armor of my clothes.

"I love you," Dominic declares and cups my face with his warm hands, gazing deep into my eyes. "May I?" he asks as his hands move down to my panties.

I nod but don't dare look away from him.

Dominic smiles and hooks his thumbs in the sides of my panties and pushes them down my legs. He then does the same thing with his boxer briefs. Looking down I'm met with a large, excited, and definitely erect cock.

Wow.

"Come." Dominic extends his hand and leads me to our bed. I sit on the edge and slide over to lie down. I hold my hand out to him.

Dominic climbs on the bed and my legs shamelessly fall open to accommodate his frame.

"Keep your eyes open and on me. Don't look away and don't close them."

"Okay," I say as I keep my gaze trained on his.

"Let me worship your body, sweetheart. Let me make love to your soul." Dominic kisses me with the utmost tenderness before trailing his wet lips and tongue down my chin, nibbling and sucking on my inflamed skin.

When he reaches my collar bone, he brushes the top of my breast then moves to my nipple. Flicking it with his tongue and sucking before he moves to the other side, teasing the damaged skin with his hot tongue.

My mind empties as my body reacts to his sensual strokes. My breathing is rapid, my skin is hot and I can feel my sex is saturated as I eagerly wait for his attention to move lower.

"Are you alright?" Dominic asks as he gently bites on my top lip then sucks it into his mouth.

"I'm wonderful," I groan as his mouth dances with mine.

"Can you feel me?"

His rigid cock is at my entrance, ready to push in.

"I can feel you." And I want to feel more.

"Keep looking at me," he whispers.

"Yes."

"Don't take your eyes off mine, I need to make sure you're okay."

"I'm more than okay," I reassure him with a smile.

"I can stop if you want me to," he says, giving me every opportunity to step away.

"Please, don't stop. Make love to me."

He returns my smile sweetly and kisses me deeply and passionately.

He pushes the tip of his cock inside me and stops, allowing my sex to adjust to his size. He keeps kissing me and pushes in a little further.

I take in a gulp of air around his mouth. It sort of pinches a little, and burns. Closing my eyes I try to concentrate on the feelings coursing through me. The feeling isn't unbearable, just a little uncomfortable. But I'm soon accepting him completely and the discomfort is disappearing, replaced by a warm, full feeling.

"Keep your eyes open, so I can tell if it gets to be too much for you."

"It's not too much, I'm just accepting you."

Dominic pushes more of himself inside me and my legs open further. He links our fingers together with our hands resting on either side of my head, and his lips don't move from mine. He stretches me and I mold around him, a perfect fit.

He thrusts all the way in, and I let out a little whimper. His mouth absorbs my cry as he continues to kiss me. My breath becomes his; his breath melts with mine. Right now, we're one complete soul. Joined together, moving together, in love together.

He lets go of my hands and leans up on his elbows, his face incredibly close to mine.

Dominic begins moving in and out of me, my own wetness coating his cock as he slides back and forth with ease. His movements are incredibly slow, almost torturous as his hips find a steady rhythm.

My nails scratch up and down his back as I let the feeling of him take my body to a new place.

My body surrenders. He owns me. Every part of me. Mind. Body. Spirit. It all belongs to him.

The tight pleasure deep in my belly grows as his drive intensifies. My heart pounds with excitement. My hot blood is frenzied by a maddening need for more.

He ravishes me with powerful, rhythmic thrusts of his hips. I lift mine off the bed to meet him and he hits a spot that increases my pleasure exponentially.

My desire for more is morphing into a raw and sinful need.

"More," I moan, moving my hips to match Dominic's pace.

He gyrates his hips as I writhe beneath him.

Dominic speeds up, and I grind hard against him. The friction of his pelvic bone against my sex is driving me to the edge.

Not once do his dark, intense orbs leave mine.

The hard knot of excitement in my belly spreads, sending prickles all over my skin.

My breath is coming out in strong, quick pants. My toes begin to tingle and I finally feel free.

With deep, fluid motions Dominic intensifies his power as he pounds into me.

A vein is sticking out on his neck, and I can tell he's holding back his own release, waiting for me. Mine is close, and the faster he bucks, the more urgent it becomes for me to just let go.

"I love you so much." Dominic's voice is strained.

He pumps faster. Now the primal need to come overtakes every other emotion.

Our bodies are so close together, sharing the same passionate dialogue, talking without words. Completely in love.

My mouth falls open as I gasp for air. Dominic leans down and kisses me. His tongue takes charge and commands me to submit. His body demands possession.

The spring inside me finally snaps and I cry out. My body trembles against Dominic. He thrusts into me hard, but holds me close to his taut, sweaty body.

He growls into my mouth, as his plunging halts, and I know he's just come inside me.

He remains inside me, rocking gently, and kisses me for a long time, flooding me with love. I feel the intense, consuming connection between us solidify. I've never felt anything like this before.

When he moves away, he slips out and lies on his back next to me, stretching an arm out toward me and pulling me to his side.

"Thank you, Dominic. I was afraid of having sex again. You made it perfect for me."

"Sweetheart, that wasn't just sex. It was so much more. We became one."

He felt it too. The love that was shared freely between us. He completely owns me now, and I own him. He said those words before, but now I really feel it.

I get up and go to the bathroom to clean up. Dominic goes to the guest bathroom. When we return to bed, I lie securely in his arms and his words replay over and over again.

"I love you," I say completely happy and satisfied as I yawn hugely.

"You gave me a gift when you first said those three words, now you've given me something I'll treasure until I die. You've given me your heart, your spirit and your body," he replies.

I smile as my eyelids droop closed.

Before long, I hear Dominic's soft snoring and my own breathing even out.

Then it hits me. I'm here, now, snuggling into the side of my lover and perfect partner. I've overcome obstacles and I'm stretching my wings, soaring to new heights.

All because…

I found the courage to open the door.

THIRTY-TWO

"*IN WHAT APPEARS TO BE ONE OF THE LARGEST AND MOST horrific cases to hit America in the last decade, prominent lawyer Oscar Shriver, policeman Michael Greene, and Rocky Adams have all been sentenced to a combined one thousand and fifty-five years in prison for the brutal rapes and murders of forty-two women. They're each eligible for parole in two hundred and three years. Oscar Shriver is the son of disgraced financiers John and Doris Shriver, who are also currently under investigation for their roles in this very disturbing case. According to court documents, Oscar Shriver was the ring leader of the gang. Michael Greene provided the break in the case after police seized his personal computer and found thousands of images of the women they had brutalized. Greene was once respected amongst his peers and known as a by-the-book police officer. Rocky Adams, a drug addict and small-time thief, was the trio's scout and hunted for their victims.*"*

Dominic switches the TV off and I'm left staring at a blank screen. Initially it was believed that thirty-six girls were taken, all tortured for the monsters' own perverse pleasure and then killed.

The irony of their sentence being handed down today is that it's the anniversary of the most horrific day of my life. It's been exactly four years since they took me, and altered my life. Exactly a year and two weeks since they arrested Oscar. His friends were arrested soon after.

"Are you alright?" Dominic asks as he places a hand on my knee.

"Do you know that today is the anniversary of the day they took me?" I keep staring at the black, reflective surface of the TV.

"Yes, I do," he confirms.

"Can we go somewhere, right now? I just need to get outside, into the sun." I turn my head and see a look of surprise quickly pass over Dominic's face. "What?" I ask, curious about his response.

"You never cease to surprise me, you know? Just when I think that you might revert back to your shy, frightened ways, you prove me wrong. And now is no exception. You, my beautiful girl, are the strongest and most courageous person that I've ever met." He reaches over to give me a hug.

Dominic offers me his hand as he stands. I place my palm in his, and he pulls me up and into his warm body.

The thrill of his heat so close to me sends a jolt of electricity all the way down to my core. His masculine scent soothes me, and his taut, solid body makes me feel so secure. He's perfect and he's the love of my life.

"Where do you want to go?" he asks as he rubs his nose across my hair. "Mmmm, you smell so nice." A deep, manly growl rumbles from within his chest. He moves my hair to the side and peppers soft, feather-light kisses from the sensitive spot behind my ear, all the way down the angle of my jaw.

My belly floods with happy, excited butterflies and my heart beats with extra force as his mouth skims my flaming skin.

"I…ah…mmm." His passionate touch distracts me, and if he keeps this up, I'm going to want to stay here. In bed.

"Where are we going, love?" he asks again and gently sucks some of my skin into his mouth. I tilt my head back to give him better access to my throat, arching my back so my breasts press into his firm chest. His hand rests on the dip at the small of my back as his other hand travels to my bottom. He grips my cheeks forcefully, pulling me closer to him.

I can feel his arousal pressing into the lower part of my belly, and my body reacts excitedly.

"Um," I'm finding it hard to form words. I want him, but I don't want to use him like this to avoid an emotional trigger. "Take me to the pond," I finally say as he continues his slow exploration of my body with his hands and mouth. He moves a half-step back to look at my face.

"Alright, I'll get us a couple of jackets." He releases me and moves away from me. The moment he leaves, I miss him and want him back.

"I'll grab two of bottles of water." I go to the kitchen while he goes upstairs.

"Ready," we say in unison as we meet by the front door. He kisses me once more and unlocks and opens the doors.

I stand looking at the alarm keypad for a moment and feel myself biting my lip and furrowing my eyebrows together. The little green light is on, telling me the alarm's off.

"What is it?" Dominic asks as he steps through the door and holds it open for me.

"I don't remember turning the alarm on last night before we went to bed."

"You don't?" He snickers.

"No I don't, did you turn it on?" I look at him and notice his cheeky smile.

"You haven't noticed then."

"Noticed what?" I say as I turn the alarm on, step over the threshold and close the heavy wooden door behind me.

"You haven't turned it on for two days."

A tingle of ice shoots up my spine, and the hairs on the back of my neck stand to attention as I take in a gulp of air. "It's been off for two days?" I whisper completely stunned at my own inattentiveness.

"Yeah, and you left the kitchen window open, too." He grins proudly.

"I did?"

We reach for each other's hand at the same moment and hook our pinkies together as we walk the garden path to our car.

"You did."

Dominic opens my car door, and waits for me to put my seatbelt on before he closes it and jogs around to the driver's side. He drapes our jackets over the back of the seat and starts the car.

Soft music fills the car, and this time I feel so different about going to the pond. The first time he took me, I was filled with dread and worry, nervous, not knowing how I would react to seeing the place where I was dumped like garbage.

Now I'm excited to see it for the beautiful site it is – perfect, the way nature intended it to be, filled with the colors of wildflowers that God's hand has touched.

When we get to the pond, I don't wait for Dominic's strong hand. I open the car door myself and step out in the small parking lot.

I stand in front of the car and look up at the utterly blue sky. The rays of the sun are warm and they touch me deeper than my skin. They illuminate the layers of my soul as I openly accept the gifts I've been given.

"You ready?" Dominic startles me from the gentle comfort I was taking from the sun.

"Yeah." We walk hand in hand out of the small parking area, and make our way through the wildflowers to the pond. The stems are a luscious green and various other vibrant colors are scattered throughout the field leading to the water.

When we get to the edge of open water, Dominic lays a picnic blanket down. I didn't even realize he was carrying it until this very moment.

Dominic lies down and props himself up on his elbows as he looks, watching a gentle breeze sending small ripples to the water's edge. I instinctively lie down and place my head on Dominic's stomach. He runs his fingers through my hair, calming me enough to make my eyelids droop. My mind relaxes, knowing that no matter where I go, he'll always be there to protect me.

"I can't believe how my life's changed," I murmur as I appreciate Dominic's gentle, loving touch.

"I knew from the moment I met you that all you needed was the right person to help you blossom. And I'm so happy that person was me."

"I'm not sure how much longer I could've held on to that life," I admit. "The best thing I ever did was turning the TV on and watching that story of the three women that were taken and kept as sex slaves for all those years. That's how I found you."

"And I'm eternally grateful that I was in the office the day you called." Dominic takes a deep breath. "Sit up," he says as he taps me on the head once.

I sit up, cross-legged, and face him as he does the same. Our knees are touching, our hands are linked tightly together, and our eyes are looking deeply into each other's.

"I'm completely in love with you, Allyn. I want to be part of everything you do. I want to be the man you need, and I want to take care of you. I want to push you when you think you can't do something, to hold your hand and tell you that you can. I want to be the man that holds you and makes love to you under the stars as you stare into my eyes and let me see deep into your soul. I want to be the only man who hears your cries of pleasure, your small whimpers as your body begins to tremble tightly around mine. I want it to be just you and me for this life and the next. I want us to be together, to love each other completely and to grow old in each other's arms. Allyn, you're the strongest and most angelic woman I've ever met. Please say you'll marry me." Dominic lets go of my hand and takes a small, pretty blue box with a white ribbon tied in a perfect bow from the pocket of his jacket.

Tears fall freely as he offers the box to me. I swipe at the saltwater that fall from my eyes and reach out slowly to take the box in my trembling hands.

"Hey, don't cry, beautiful girl. I love you, and you love me. That's all that matters in our world."

"I do love you, so much more than I ever thought was possible."

I don't untie the bow. I don't need to look at the ring to know that it's perfect. Dominic chose it, so under the lid will be a rare beauty, shining brightly and conveying a deep meaning. Because that is what Dominic does. He takes the ordinary and turns it into the extraordinary.

"Yes," I whisper as I look into his eyes.

"I love you," he says as his mouth collides with mine.

He possesses me, owns me, and his love has led me to a life less broken.

EPILOGUE

Rocky Adams

In One Section of Cell Block C, 5.55pm

I'VE BEEN HERE FOR TWO DAYS NOW, AND NOTHING HAS happened. I keep to myself and have only copped one beating.

I've sussed out the dealer here and I've watched him. He's protected by a strong formation of prison thugs.

But I'm dying for one little hit, just enough to get me though these next few days. I've gone too fucking long without anything. Of course, the motherfucking jail doesn't allow us to bring in anything. Jail isn't supposed to be a comfortable place, but it's fucking tough as shit. I need a hit before I lose my goddamn mind.

I carefully approach the table where King J's sitting. His goons form a barrier around him and stop me from advancing any further.

"Can I see him, please?" Fuck the 'please' bullshit, but if it gets me a line, I'll do it.

"Let him through," I hear the deep grumble of King J from behind the huge buffoon in front of me.

The guy steps aside and King J motions for me to come closer.

"What do you want?" he asks gruffly.

"I hear you're the man to come to when I need something to take the edge off."

"Fuck off before I beat you to death," he says disdainfully and looks away from me, totally disregarding my presence.

One of his henchmen starts pushing me away.

"Please, I just need a little." I shamelessly beg for anything he can give me.

"Wait," he says and the gorilla takes his hands off me. I brush his hands away and give him a 'eat shit' look as I step closer to the table.

"Follow me," King J says as he stands and starts walking toward the cells.

I follow eagerly, 'cause I can't fucking wait to get a taste of the magic white powder that makes me come alive.

We get to his cell. As he stands with his back to the wall, his army forms a protective barrier around us, blocking us from the guards' sight.

Fuck, what have I gotten myself into?

"What are you gonna do for me in exchange for what you need?" he asks as he crosses his arms in front of his massive chest.

"Um, I don't know. What do you want?"

"My cock needs sucking," he says flatly.

Whoa – I don't do guys.

"I'm not gay," I say, taking a step back from him.

"Neither am I, but my cock needs someone's lips wrapped around it. Seeing as my spine's not made of rubber, and you want something I have, you'd best get on your knees and wrap that pretty little mouth of yours around my dick."

"Are you fucking serious?" I ask, completely horrified.

He shrugs. "Do you want a hit or do you a want a beating? Either way, I don't care. Your choice."

I close my eyes and swallow the huge lump in my throat. Bile starts creeping up behind it and will soon be all over the cement floor. But fuck, just one little taste will be enough to get me right.

Slowly I sink to my knees, close my eyes tight and open my mouth. I feel his cock slide in and I dry retch while trying to stop myself from gagging.

He grabs the sides of my head and holds me still while he fucks my mouth hard.

Roughly, he keeps slamming into me as I gag. Finally, I feel his cum spurt down my throat. He locks his hands around the back of my head and holds me there until I swallow all of it.

Disgusting, salty, vile-tasting shit, that is.

I sit back on the floor and I'm disgusted with myself for stooping so low.

Thank God it's over. I'll never do that shit again.

When I look up, King J has placed the smallest line I've ever seen on the back of his hand. It's not even half a line, maybe only a third.

"What the fuck? I just sucked you off and that's all you're giving me?" I say angrily as I stand and point to the pathetic excuse for a line on his hand.

"You want a full line, you have to bend over," he says, completely confident.

"I have to what?" I ask, stunned.

"You want a full line? Then you let me fuck you up your ass."

What the fuck?

"I'm not gay," I say again in the smallest of voices, more to convince myself than King J.

"Neither am I." His face is completely devoid of emotion.

Fuck. I take the step toward him and snort the shit off his hand. If I'm going to do this, I need to be flying so at least I can forget.

I drop my pants, turn around and bend over for King J.

He rams into me without warning, without even spitting on his cock first to ease the way. I scream out in pain as he hammers hard into my ass.

The torment is barbarous as he continues to slam into me. He grips my hips, and I'm about to lose everything in my stomach as he angrily pounds into me.

He comes deep in my ass. I feel used, degraded and disgusting.

I pull my pants up and turn around to see a full line on the back of his hand.

I snort it all up and lick his hand, getting every last particle of powder left there. I just got fucked in the ass for it, so I may as well take what I deserve.

I turn to walk out of the cell, but my asshole burns with severe, brutal pain with every move I make.

"This time every day, you meet me here," King J says.

Fuck, what have I gotten myself into?

EPILOGUE

Michael Greene

In Another Section of Cell Block C, 5.55pm

"**W**ELL, LOOK WHO WE HAVE HERE," I TURN AROUND AND SEE six guys surrounding me. I recognize all of them as guys who may have taken a beating or two from me when I arrested them.

They've trapped me in a quiet corner of the cellblock. I hold my hands up in surrender and try to push past them.

"Hey, it's that dirty cop that likes to kill pretty young girls," another one of them says as he takes a menacing step toward me.

"We're all the same in here, boys," I say as I try to brush past the tight-knit group of guys closing in on me.

"Ha, seems he thinks he's the same as us."

The first punch lands on the side of my head, stunning me and knocking me off balance.

The next punch follows rapidly after the first and I know immediately I stand no chance against them.

The third punch hits my stomach and a swift kick behind my knees puts me down.

Feet keep kicking into me, fists pound hard into every part of my body.

I feel a snap in my arm and I scream out in agony. Someone laughs roughly and the beating gets more aggressive.

I try to protect my head but I can't move my arms. They feel so heavy and the pain is unbearable. One of them turns me on my back, and the barrage of blows continues to intensify.

Finally I get turned on my stomach again. They prop my chin out, fully extending my neck.

In that one moment, I know what they're going to do to me.

"I'm so sorry for all the girls I hurt," I whisper as my tears drip to the cold concrete beneath me.

A hard shoe stomps on my neck.

Goodbye, Faith.

EPILOGUE

Oscar Shriver

In A Different Section of Cell Block C, 5.55pm

"**TWO THOUSAND A WEEK,**" HE SAYS AS HE LOOKS AT ME.

"Two thousand a week?" I ask in sheer shock.

"Protection is two thousand a week. You're the hot-shot attorney that mommy and daddy kept bailing out. So for two thousand a week, I'll protect you." This guy is huge, and by huge, I mean he's easily twice my size, scarred, and scary as fuck.

"Who do I need protection from?" I ask. I'll find out who I need to worry about so I can barter with them individually.

"First there're the white supremacists. They don't like people raping white girls. Then there are the Asians. They don't like Asian girls being tortured. And there's the black pack who don't like colored girls being mauled and cut up. Then there's me. I don't like rapists, period. So two thousand a week will protect you against them, and me, for now."

"I don't have that sort of money," I say earnestly. "All my assets are frozen, and my parents are under investigation so they can't get me any money either."

"Hmmm, seems you have a problem then." He smiles menacingly. "This is really your only option. I'm a reasonable man, so I'll give you twenty-four hours to give me your answer. Ha, that is if you survive that long. I heard the blacks talking with the whites, seems now they've got a common goal – killing you." He turns around and leaves me, alone.

This is so much worse than hell.

I'm truly fucked in here. If I survive that long. Fuck.

Who the hell am I going to turn to? The only person I know that's not in shit as deep as me is Dominic, but he won't accept my calls.

I tried to call him yesterday, but he's changed his number. He's changed all of his numbers.

I'm so fucking alone.

EPILOGUE

Six Years Later

"**W**HERE ARE WE GOING?" I ASK DOMINIC AS I TRY TO PEEK from beneath the silken blindfold he's tied tight around my head.

"Are you trying to cheat?" he says playfully.

"No. Well, yes."

"It's not too much further. You'll just have to wait and see."

The car turns and the road becomes very bumpy, like we're going down a trail of sorts.

"Come on, we've been in the car for hours," I whine and draw out the last word.

"Mrs. Shriver, you are officially a pain in the ass."

"Daddy said a naughty word," Chloe chimes in from the back seat.

"Yes, Daddy did and he shouldn't have. Sorry Chloe," Dominic tells our eight-year-old daughter.

Chloe is a blessing. Dominic took me to China for our honeymoon, and while we were there, we visited an orphanage to offer our help. The most beautiful little girl came up to me and sat on my lap. Her right eye had been gouged out when she was a baby, her own short life a horrific case of torture. She placed her hand on my left eye and smiled at me.

Though language and age was a barrier, she was silently telling me what I already knew – that we were the same.

Dominic and I fought hard, jumped over every hurdle and followed every instruction we were given. Three months later, we bought Chloe home with us.

She's our rainbow and the most perfect daughter, completing our beautiful family.

As I reflect back on the miracle of Chloe, I can't help but think how truly blessed Dominic and I are. Even though Dominic never spoke to his parents again, mine have been an integral part of our family. They've been nothing but supportive of us, and when we adopted Chloe they became the most appreciative and supportive doting grandparents.

Dominic and I are also close to Faith and her husband, Joshua, and their twin sons. We stood beside Faith and Joshua on their wedding day, and we were honored when they asked us to be godparents to their boys.

Life really has taken a different direction in the last eight years. I was once held captive by fear, only living my life in beige. Now I live with brilliant, vibrant colors, all because I found the courage to open my door.

The car engine shutting off snaps me out of my reverie. "Stay there 'til I get you out," Dominic says to me. "Now remember what we talked about, Chloe?"

"Oh yes I do, Daddy. I promise not to say a word."

"Good girl." Dominic gets out and shuts his door.

What is going on?

I hear Chloe's door shut and the silence in the car tells me that I've been left alone.

I'm tempted to lift the blindfold, but I know that Dominic's been planning whatever this is for months, and I don't want to ruin his surprise.

He disappears when his phone rings, he hides his tablet, and once he yelled at me when I was doing laundry because I was checking his pockets for anything that wasn't supposed to go through the wash. He bolted in and grabbed something from his shirt pocket, kissed me on the forehead and ran out again.

"Okay, give me your hand," he says when he opens my door. I offer him my right hand and he entwines our fingers and helps me out. "The ground is a little unsteady, so we'll go slow." He wraps an arm around my waist.

The fresh spring air is so crisp and vibrant, and the sound of different birds singing together is heavenly. I breathe deeply loving the freshness.

"Three more steps and we're going to stop," he says.

Chloe is by my side and I can feel her holding onto my skirt as I take those daunting three steps.

"Okay. I'm going to take the blindfold off now." His hands are at the back of my head as he unties the smooth piece of material.

It skims with a whisper across my skin as he removes it, and my eyes blink a few times to adjust to the brightness of the day.

In front of me stands a tall, regal horse, with dark brown hair and black pointy ears. He's as beautiful and stunning as I remember him to be.

Mr. Boss.

Tears fall, and I start to breathe heavier. I'm completely stunned.

"How did you find him?" I ask as I step slowly toward the beautiful animal who's calmly munching the grass in the paddock.

"It was a little hard, but I did."

I swipe at the tears, a lump of happiness lodged in my throat.

"Are you sad, Mommy?"

"Oh no, darling I'm not sad at all. I'm really, really happy. What you and your daddy have done for me is just perfect. Thank you." I kiss the top of her head, and turn to kiss Dominic too. "Are you sure it's okay that we're here? The owners may not like us trespassing like this," I say to Dominic.

"Oh, the owners aren't going to mind," he says with that cheeky smile. "Because, as of yesterday, we now own this land and everything on it, including Mr. Boss." His face beams with pride.

My heart thumps with the biggest jolt of joy and love I've ever experienced. I throw my arms around Dominic and kiss him with so much vigor and intoxication I almost knock him down.

"Tell her, Daddy! Tell her now!" Chloe shrieks in excitement as she pats Mr. Boss through the fence.

"Tell me what?" I ask as I pull back to look at Dominic.

"The adoption agency called this morning. They've found us a baby girl. We're going to meet her tonight," he says as he pulls me into a tight embrace.

"We're adding a second perfect daughter to our beautiful family," I squeal in excitement. As I reach out for Chloe it's then that I see him, the beautiful blue jay soaring freely through the crystal clear skies.

CRISIS HOTLINE NUMBERS
IF HELP IS NEEDED

USA

Suicide Prevention and Crisis Hotline:
Available 24/7/365
1-800-273-8255

AUSTRALIA

Lifeline:
Available 24/7/365
131114

UK

Supportline:
01708765200

ACKNOWLEDGEMENTS

My dear family who always support me: **Andrew**, **Grace**, **Olivia** and **Mum**.

To beautiful friends who I can count on for whatever I need: **Tina**, **Melissa** and **Lindy**.

My PIBC, who's been incredibly patient with as my head runs in different directions: **Heather**.

A mentor and a treasured friend: **Sue**.

A new editor who came to me at the best of times: **Debi**.

My new proof-reader who's happy to read everything I give him: **Al**.

My beta readers, who pushed me and told me the parts they loved and the parts that were MEH and needed to be fixed: **Heather**, **Mandy** and **Brittany**. (Welcome to the family girls.)

My very new street team, you ladies are truly fantastic for being part of the journey with me (to many more books): **Shona** and **Hetty** (my admin), **Trish**, **Mandy**, **Shanda**, **Jennifer**, **Patricia**, **Maureen**, **Jess**, **Rachel**, **Amy** and **Brittany**.

To a very special friend who's believed in me from my very first book, HiT 149. The execution may have sucked (less sucky now) but you read it and remained very courteous and professional in your critique. You've become more than my promo chick, and I think you know that. Thank you, for everything, **Hetty**.

Thank you to the blogs who continue to support me, but a very special mention to: **Bestellers and Beststellars of Romance, Panty Dropping Book Blog** and **Kitty Kats Crazy About Books**. These three are always there, and without hesitation will do what they can for me. And for that, I'm eternally grateful – because without you, us Indie authors would still be chasing our tails.

However, the most important thank you must come to **you**. The reader. Thank you for supporting me, for telling your friends and for doing what you do. Read!

Like me on FaceBook at Margaret McHeyzer Author
Email: hit_149@yahoo.com

MORE FROM ME

Jaeger Dalton wants the land that was promised to him.

Phoenix Ward isn't about to let anyone take Freedom Run away from her.

He'll protect what's his.

She'll protect what's hers.

Jaeger is an arrogant ass, but he wants nothing more than Phoenix.

Phoenix is stubborn and headstrong, and she wants Jaeger out of her life.

Her father lost the family farm to gambling debts, but Jaeger isn't the only one who has a claim to the property.

Sometimes it's best to let things go.

But sometimes it's better to fight until the very end.

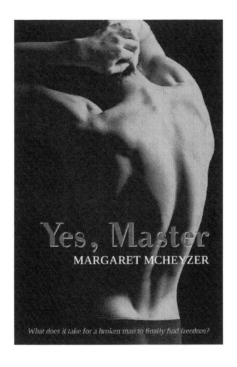

**THIS NOVEL CONTAINS DISTRESSING CONTENT.
IT IS ONLY SUITED FOR READERS OVER 18.**

ALSO CONTAINS M/M, M/M/F, M/F AND F/F SCENES.

My uncle abused me.

I was 10 years old when it started.

At 13 he told me I was no longer wanted because I had started to develop.

At 16 I was ready to kill him.

Today, I'm broken.

Today, I only breathe to survive.

My name's Sergeant Major Ryan Jenkins and today, I'm ready to tell you my story

HiT Series

Must be read in order

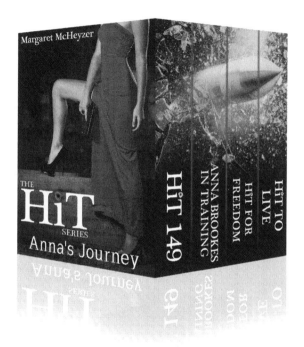

HiT 149

Anna Brookes is the most dangerous woman that you hope you will never know. Her life of danger started the day she turned 15.

The thirteen years that follow shapes her life to become the most deadly and lethal woman. HiT 149 becomes her most difficult target.

Does she pull the trigger or does she risk becoming the target herself?

Anna Brookes in Training
(HiT #1.5)

Imagine watching your Father die in front of you because two men were sent to take you. The two men were sent by Roman Murphy, the boss of Hunter Inc. The sole job of Hunter Inc. is to train and produce assassins.

Anna Brookes, a 15 year old girl with a love and panache for precision and handling of weapons was sought out by Hunter Inc.

One evening she encounters Lukas, a man she saves but a man who ultimately goes on to save her.

The months that follow sees Anna's intuition heightened and defined.

She is forced to deal with techniques that no ordinary 15 year old girl should ever encounter in their lives.

HiT for Freedom
(HiT #2)

Anna Brookes also known by her Professional name 15, did what she had never done before.

She didn't kill her target, HiT 149.

HiT 149 better known as Ben Pearson did something he had never done before.

He fell in love with Anna Brookes.

In Hit for Freedom, the sequel to HiT 149, a nemesis so powerful, terrifying and frightening is threatening the safety of Anna's love, Ben and his hometown, St Cloud.

15 must deal with a force that may be too dangerous even for her skilled ways. With limited information on her new HiT, she willingly infiltrates his trust to acquire the knowledge she needs to implode the operations of the deadly man.

HiT to Live
(HiT #3)

Anna Brookes, AKA 15, held the title of the girl with the golden aim. Through dedication and training she quickly rose to be the best assassin in the world.

But no amount of preparation could guard her heart against falling in love.

Anna's armor was severely crumpled when she met Ben Pearson, the one man that managed to get under her skin and stay there.

When Katsu Vang, a powerful player in the Yakuza, became a threat to Ben, Anna did the one thing she knew best—she went into assassin mode and fought the problem at the source.

Katsu Vang proved to be an admirable adversary that even Anna couldn't take down on her own. Because of her undercover intel work, Anna became a target for Katsu. She was sold into the sex trade and continuously injected with heroin until her body was hopelessly addicted.

Ben Pearson was hiding behind his own mask, which finally dropped as his true identity was revealed to Anna in HiT for Freedom.

Ophelia is Ben's right hand at the job he held as a front. Ophelia has her own vendetta and wants her mother's killer brought to justice.

Katsu has vanished but his power still poses an imminent threat to all concerned.

Anna Brookes is the common link between all the players…

The one woman that can put all the pieces together…

And the one woman that can tear everything down.

He's lived a life of high society and privilege; he chose to follow in his father's footsteps and become a Senator.

She's lived a life surrounded with underworld activity; she had no choice but to follow in her father's footsteps and take on the role of Mob Boss.

He wants to stamp out organized crime and can't be bought off.

She's the ruthless and tough Mob Boss where in her world all lines are blurred.

Their lives are completely different, two walks of life on the opposite ends of the law.

Being together doesn't make sense.

But being apart isn't an option

Ellie Andrews has been receiving tutoring from Blake McCarthy for three years to help her improve her grades so she can get into one of the top universities to study law. And she's had a huge crush on him since she can remember.

Blake McCarthy is the geek at school that's had a crush on Ellie since the day he met her.

In their final tutoring session, Blake and Ellie finally become brave enough to take the leap of faith.

But, life has other plans and rips them apart.Six years later Blake and his best friends Ben and Billy have built a successful internet platform company 3BCubed, while Ellie is a successful and hardworking lawyer specializing in Corporate Law.

3BCubed is being threatened with a devastatingly large plagiarism case and when it lands on their lawyers desk, it's handed to the new Corporate Lawyer to handle and win.

Coincidence or perhaps fate will see Blake and Ellie pushed back together.

Binary Law will have Blake and Ellie propelled into a life that's a whirl wind of catastrophic events and situations where every emotion will be touched. Hurt will be experienced, happiness will be presented and love will be evident. But is that enough for Blake and Ellie be able to live out their own happily ever after?

Made in the USA
Charleston, SC
07 August 2014